THE
QUESTION
OF
MIRACLES

THE QUESTION OF MIRACLES

ELANA K. ARNOLD

Houghton Mifflin Harcourt
Boston   New York

www.hmhco.com

Text set in ITC Cheltenham Std.

The Library of Congress has cataloged the hardcover edition as follows:
Arnold, Elana K.
The question of miracles / by Elana K. Arnold.
p. cm.
Summary: Unhappy about moving from sunny California to rainy Corvallis,
Oregon, and grieving over the death of her best friend, sixth-grader Iris looks
for a miracle and may find one in new friend Boris.
[1. Miracles—Fiction. 2. Grief—Fiction. 3. Moving, Household—Fiction. 4.
Friendship—Fiction. 5. Corvallis (Or.)—Fiction.] I. Title.
PZ7.A73517Qu 2015
[Fic]—dc23
2014000738

ISBN: 978-0-544-33464-9 hardcover
ISBN: 978-0-544-66852-2 paperback

Manufactured in the United States of America
DOC 10 9 8 7 6 5 4 3 2 1
4500579380

For Alex Kuczynski, my dad, who makes me feel like a miracle

Iris stood inside the great big double-wide doorway of the gymnasium-slash-auditorium-slash-lunchroom. It was crazy in there—track marks from wet, muddy shoes crisscrossed the lacquered wooden floor. A miserable teacher sopped up spilled milk right in the middle of everything. Three more teachers wandered the perimeter, keeping an eye on the whole scene, shushing kids when they got too loud, telling a pair of boys to "Cut out the horseplay!" when they started tossing some girl's orange back and forth over her head.

The acoustics were terrible; the voices from the crowd of kids inside made Iris feel like her brain was an apple on y, tipping over and knocking against the side of her head.

Back home in California, no one ever ate lunch indoors—lunchtime was a strictly outdoor activity. On the two or three rainy days each year, they'd eat in their classroom while the teacher played a movie, but other than that, they ate outside at concrete picnic tables, just to the right of a big open field. It was humane. There was room to breathe.

But that was back home. Here in Oregon, where it had rained literally *every day* since they'd parked the moving van in the long gravel driveway of the farmhouse Iris's dad had bought sight unseen (except for the video tour on the real estate agent's website), school lunch had to be consumed indoors.

It was another reason to hate it here. As if Iris didn't have a long enough list already. Along with the ridiculous noise of the reverberating voices, there was also the smell—the musty, mildewy, earthy stench of too much rain, socks that never did dry out completely, and wet hair.

But she couldn't just stand there all day. The other kids were starting to turn and stare at her.

There was a table at the far side of the gymnasium, just under a basketball hoop, that wasn't completely crowded. Iris headed there, ignoring the questioning glances on the other kids' faces. Ignoring the occasional smile, too. Ignoring everything.

And when she slid into an empty spot near the end of a bench, she ignored the kid sitting next to her—a mouth breather she remembered seeing in her Social Studies class before lunch. She *felt* him there, though—the aura of his curly hair, the wet-wool scent of his red and blue striped pullover, the weight of him taking up space.

This was Iris's first day of school, even though September was almost over. Her dad had wanted her to be homeschooled, which had sounded like a good idea to Iris—she wasn't in a big hurry to be around a lot of people—but after two weeks of trying to do schoolwork at their kitchen table, with her dad sipping coffee and looking over her shoulder, Iris had insisted that her parents enroll her at Linus Pauling Middle School. At home in California, sixth grade meant being the oldest kids at the elementary school. Here, it meant being among the youngest, lumped into the gym at lunchtime with teenagers whose bodies smelled like grownups and who looked at each other in a way that Iris didn't have all the words for but knew she didn't like.

Iris pulled out her lunch. The boy from Social Studies class was eating a microwaved burrito. It smelled worse than the packed bodies, worse than the rain. Iris could hear him chewing.

To block out the sound, she took a big bite of her apple and listened to it crunch between her teeth. Iris put all of her attention into eating that apple—bite, chew-chew-chew-chew, swallow. Bite.

"You really like apples," said Burrito Boy.

Iris ignored him.

"You like the red ones, too, or just the green kind?"

"The red ones are mealy," Iris answered begrudgingly. It was one thing to ignore a tablemate; another thing entirely to ignore a direct question. She didn't feel like being *that* rude.

"Yeah, I think so too," said the boy. "You ever try a Pink Lady?"

Iris shook her head.

"You should," he said, enthusiastic now. "They're the best. They're crisp like a green apple, but sweeter, like a red. Kind of tangy, too." Then he added, "My name's Boris."

Finally, Iris turned to look at the boy next to her. She wondered if he was teasing her, making fun of her in some way she wasn't quite catching on to.

But his expression was wide open, earnest. His dark brown curls rioted around his face, there was a flush in his round cheeks, his eyes—as dark as his hair—weren't laughing at her, but waited eagerly for her response.

Everything about him was doglike—the way he sort of sat forward in his chair, the way he waited for her to answer, the way his eyes stayed on her face.

Unfortunately for him, Iris was a *cat* person.

She turned away. "Thanks for the recommendation," she said. "I'll ask my dad to pick some up."

She unwrapped the sandwich her dad had packed for her that morning—egg salad. At least there was that.

"Your dad does the shopping at your house, huh?" In typical doglike fashion, Boris didn't take the hint that Iris was done talking. Not seeming to care that she didn't answer, Boris continued. "My mom's the grocery shopper for our family. But I make her take me along whenever I'm around, because she buys all the wrong stuff. Like plain Cheerios instead of the honey kind. Low-fat milk instead of whole."

Iris didn't tell Boris that her dad did the shopping because her mother was busy working at the university, doing important research, or that her dad was actually a really good grocery shopper, and a good cook, and even a good gardener. That was the thing her dad had been the most excited about, when they moved—the gardening. "Can't grow anything in that sandy beach soil. When we get settled in, I'm going to grow all the produce we can eat. Self-sufficient, that's what we'll be," he'd told them both—Iris and her mom—on the sixteen-hour drive up the coast of California, through half the length of Oregon, and plop into the heart of the Willamette Valley. That's what Corvallis *meant*, even—Heart of the Valley. And the town was surrounded by farmland. Cows and great big rolls of green alfalfa.

But it had rained every day since they'd moved, and her dad still hadn't braved the weather to dig his garden.

Iris tried not to feel smug.

Around her, the other kids were finishing their lunches. And they all seemed to know the routine; when a table emptied, they signaled one of the teachers, who came over to fold the table. Then the kids would help push it to the far side of the gymnasium.

A tall, skinny girl with long, skinny braids rolled out a cart full of balls. Dodge balls and basketballs.

A boy with feet as big as Iris's father's came over and stared at her and Boris. "You almost finished?" he asked. "We wanna play."

Iris looked up. Above her was the basketball net, strung onto a red metal hoop. The net was made of thin off-white rope, knotted and tied in a series of loops. Each of the topmost loops attached to one of the hooks that rimmed the hoop—fifteen of them, Iris counted. From there the net narrowed in a series of diamonds down to a limp, not-quite-circular mouth that yawned at her.

Iris shoved the crusts of her sandwich and her apple core into her lunch bag. She hadn't even opened her orange juice. She stood and watched as the teacher collapsed the table, as it contorted in on itself.

There was a loud bang behind her, and Iris gasped, jumped a little. She felt her heart pound, her stomach sicken.

"It's just a stack of trays that fell over," Boris said.

"Over there." He pointed across the gym, where a dozen pea-green lunch trays were scattered across the floor. In the midst of them, two boys played around, one trying to knock a baseball cap off the other's head. "You okay?" asked Boris. He looked concerned, earnest. Doglike.

Iris nodded as she grabbed her backpack and turned away, hurrying out of the gym.

It was a terrible school, Iris told herself. And she hated basketball.

2

Iris's house was the last stop of the school bus route. They had added the stop just for her.

When she first climbed on board, Iris took a moment to look around. It was just as she'd always expected a school bus to be, just as they always looked in movies — double rows of black bench seats, an arched metal ceiling, those metal-rimmed windows that could open up or down or both, with one pane of glass disappearing behind the other.

Like the gymnasium — and the classroom, and the hallway — the bus smelled damp. And as more kids shoved in behind her, forcing Iris down the aisle to the back of the bus, the closed windows started to fog over with the students' combined warm, moist breath.

Iris slumped onto a bench two rows up from the last and parked her backpack next to her to discourage any potential seatmates.

It worked, which Iris found both grimly satisfying and somehow disappointing. She'd never ridden the bus back home, but she'd always had a seatmate; she and her best friend, Sarah, had been across-the-street neighbors, and Iris's dad and Sarah's mom had taken turns driving them to school and home again. Sarah would have thought the bus was wonderful, with its lack of seat belts and double-hung windows and springy vinyl-covered benches.

The bus lurched forward with a screech of wet tires and a crescendo of laughter and chatter all around. Iris looked toward the window, but the tears in her eyes and her breath condensing on the glass obscured the never-ending scape of green, which was just fine with her.

It was beautiful, this stupid place. It was all the rain. It made everything lush and green, but it also made it impossible to explore anything. Because the rain never stopped.

She hated it, even if it was beautiful. So what to its stupid beauty? Seal Beach had been beautiful too, in a different way. A usable way. The long, smooth sand beach, the straight wooden pier with the burger joint way out at the end of it. The smell of fish, the whisker-thin fishing lines up and down the pier. Iris had loved Seal Beach. She loved its name, the image it conjured—sleek seals sunning on the beach, rolling over onto their backs and stretching in the warm sand.

The bus pulled to the side of the road for its first stop, and the doors cranked open. Half a dozen kids spilled down the stairs and into the rain, all of them pulling up the hoods of their slickers but not one of them opening an umbrella.

"They'll know you're not from around here if you carry an umbrella," Iris's dad had said that morning, before he'd driven her to school. He had to take her that first day so that he could fill out all the forms, sign things.

"I *want* them to know I'm not from here," Iris said. Her voice sounded mean to her own ears. "*Here* is stupid."

The doors swung closed, and the bus was on its way. A row up and across the aisle, two girls whispered closely. For one moment Iris wondered if they were talking about her. But then the girl next to the window scrawled two sets of initials surrounded by a poorly drawn heart onto the steamed-up glass, and the other girl shrieked and reached over to erase it with her palm. Then they both turned to see if the boy across from them was watching, and they collapsed into laughter.

It was obnoxious.

They *could* have been talking about her. All day it had seemed like everyone was looking at Iris.

At the next stop, more than half of the remaining kids disembarked, including the boy she'd sat next to at lunch . . . Boris, was it? Those two silly girls got off too, and one of them bumped into Boris, knocking the paperback he held to the ground. He picked it up, sopping wet. He shook his head and shot the girls an annoyed glance, but neither of them even noticed.

They all walked toward a large, circular housing tract. All the houses looked pretty new. They had identical roofs and front doors, and exteriors painted various shades of pink and beige.

It wasn't all that different from the neighborhood Iris and Sarah had shared back home. Except that here all the walls were streaked dark with rain, the tiles spotted with moss.

The rain came down harder and harder, pounding against the roof of the bus, as they made their next few stops. Then it was just Iris and the bus driver, and it felt weird to be sitting all alone in the back, so Iris grabbed her backpack and weaved up to the front, sitting down behind the driver.

The bus driver looked into the rearview mirror and caught Iris's gaze. Iris had assumed the bus driver was wearing a hooded jacket or something—she hadn't really paid attention when she'd boarded the bus—but now she saw that the driver was a dark-skinned woman, and that she was wearing one of those head coverings that Muslims wear.

"You're new," said the driver.

"Uh-huh."

"Do you like it so far?"

Iris wished she had just stayed at the back of the bus. Why did people always want to *talk* to her? She shrugged, then realized that the driver wouldn't be able to see that, so she said, "It's okay," which was a lie.

The driver laughed. "It was hard for me to get used to, when I moved here," she said. "Where I come from, it is hot and dry. No rain like this, all the time." She gestured with her left hand, the right clutching the gigantic steering wheel. Iris saw that she had pretty hands, and that she wore a gold band on her ring finger.

"Your folks didn't want to live closer to town," the driver said, but it wasn't a question, so Iris didn't answer.

Then the bus driver seemed to get that Iris didn't much feel like talking. She didn't seem insulted or anything.

Finally they pulled up to the beginning of Iris's long driveway.

The driver stopped the bus and pushed the lever that swung open the doors. "I'm sorry, but I can't take the bus up to the house. School rules."

The rain fell in constant sheets. Iris sighed, then stood and lifted her backpack onto her back, over both shoulders. She fished her collapsible umbrella out of her jacket pocket.

"It's okay," she said again. "Thanks for the ride."

"Not a problem," said the driver.

Then there was nothing else to say, no reason to delay heading into the rain, and anyway, it only seemed to be coming down heavier the longer she waited, so Iris gave a halfhearted wave behind her and descended the four steps, her rain boots crunching the gravel as she thrust open the umbrella, latched it into place, and ran up the driveway.

She held the umbrella half in front of her like a shield, which made it hard to see where she was going, but the rain seemed to be coming from all directions rather than straight down, so that was the only way the umbrella was even a help at all.

She wasn't far from the front porch when the wind suddenly shifted. A gust stronger than she was ripped the umbrella from her hands and flipped the canopy inside out. Her umbrella tumbled off the driveway and into the overgrown grass, like a broken bird. Without meaning to, Iris stopped, open-mouthed, staring after it as it tumbled on and on, end over end. And then a crack of lightning split the sky, and Iris ran for the house, banging up the wooden porch steps and through the door, which she slammed behind her.

She stood and dripped the rain onto the carpet runner in the front hall, breathing sharply.

"Iris?" called her dad. He poked his head in from the

kitchen and raised his eyebrows at her. He had terribly expressive eyebrows. "For God's sake, Iris, take off those boots and your jacket before you flood the place."

His words brought Iris back into her body, and she tore open her raincoat, hearing the seven satisfying pops that accompanied the snaps. She hung the coat on the coat rack and pulled off her rain boots, setting them by the door.

Her dad reappeared, this time with two towels, and he tossed one to Iris before spreading the second beneath the raincoat to soak up the water it still dripped.

"We're going to have to devise a better system," he said, but Iris recognized his tone to mean that he was thinking aloud rather than talking to her, and so she said nothing.

She appreciated that her dad had built a fire, although if he hadn't moved her way out here to the middle of nowhere, no fire would have been necessary. Now, away from Seal Beach, she realized that their old fireplace had really been ornamental; any fire they built was for mood rather than a need for warmth.

Poor Charles skulked as close to the fire as he could. His gray-skinned flank pressed almost against the fire grate, his long, skinny tail curled into a loop against his side. Charles was Iris's only pet. She was allergic to cats but desperately in love with them, and so her parents had bought her Charles for her ninth birthday, two years ago. He was a sphynx—a hairless cat. An abomination, Iris's dad sometimes joked, but Charles looked so pitiful here, huddled up beside the fire, that Iris felt especially sorry for him.

Iris pulled off her sweater because it was damp and used her toes to peel her socks off, inside out, and then perched on the hearth, careful not to disturb Charles. She reached out to stroke his back, down the knobby path of his spine, but her hand must have been freezing because a wave of wrinkles tightened over his gray alien skin and he leaped down, his tail unfurling and pointing into the air as he disappeared into the kitchen.

Now it was just her—just Iris—alone by the fire. She sighed and slumped down, turning first one way and then the other in an effort to get warm. In the kitchen, her father whistled a song, and she heard the thud of the knife as he chopped something for dinner. After a while, Charles slunk back into the living room and jumped onto her lap. Her hands were warmer now, and the cat allowed her to scratch his ears, rub his shoulders a little. He didn't purr, though; Iris wondered if he was conserving his energy.

The fire was working, warming her through, and Iris considered finding the remote control so that she could watch some TV. But she didn't want to disturb Charles again, so she just sat there underneath him. He closed his uncanny blue eyes and settled into her more fully.

Little around her was familiar; in an effort to embrace the idea of a "fresh start," her parents had thrown a giant yard sale, practically giving away all their furniture—the couch, the kitchen table, the sideboard that had held their knickknacks and holiday china.

Even the holiday china.

"It's silly to have a whole set of dishes for just one day a year, don't you think?" her mother had said to Iris, just before she sold the set to an enormously pregnant Asian lady.

So there wasn't much in this room to remind Iris of home—a leather ottoman her dad had refused to get rid of; a standing lamp with a Tiffany shade that had been a wedding present to her parents; Charles.

And, of course, there was Sarah's ghost.

ris's dad made lasagna for dinner. Iris ate it begrudgingly; she felt like punishing him for her horrible day by ignoring her meal, but it was just so *good*—aromatic meaty tomato sauce, melted stringy cheese, layers of cooked-just-right flat noodles.

There was a salad, too, which Iris found easier to ignore. She didn't like to eat more than one thing at a time, and rather than fill her plate with salad when the lasagna was gone, she spooned out a second hot serving.

Iris's mom had gotten home right before dinner was served. When she banged through the front door and dripped her share of rain onto the hall runner, Iris's dad repeated his routine with the towels. "You girls have no appreciation for the importance of maintaining a dry floor," he said, clearly irritated.

But Iris's mom just laughed and shook her wet hair at him. "I think you're going to have to get used to a certain base level of dampness," she said as she loosened the belt of her raincoat.

Iris admired her mother's fashion sense. She was a big woman—tall, but also broad-shouldered and full of soft curves—large breasts, a belly that Charles loved to sleep on in the evenings when they watched TV together, a rear end that ensured she would always be perfectly comfortable without a seat cushion.

And she loved to wear frilly things. Even her raincoat was pretty—light pink and yellow with an ornamental puff capping each sleeve and a ruffle along the bottom edge.

Secretly, Iris liked frills and puffs too. But she always felt silly wearing them, like she was trying to get attention, which she wasn't.

At the table, her dad poured dark red wine for himself and Iris's mom. Iris had milk.

"Did you make any friends today?" asked her mother as she sipped the wine.

Iris shook her head, but her mother looked so disappointed that she said, "Well, I sat next to this kid Boris at lunch. He was all right." Her mother's mood seemed to brighten considerably. Iris turned to her dad. "Have you ever heard of Pink Ladies?"

"Is that a punk band?" he asked.

"No. It's a kind of apple. Boris said they're the best." Iris tried to remember his exact words. "Boris told me that they're crisp like a green apple, but sweeter, like a red. And tangy." She shrugged.

"You talked about *apples* with the boy?" Iris's mom seemed to find this amusing.

"What *should* we have talked about? I don't know any of these people. They don't know me. They *shouldn't* know me. I should still be back home in Seal Beach."

Her parents exchanged a worried glance, and her mom said, "I'm sorry. Of course you can talk about apples. You can talk about anything you want."

"Well, thanks for your permission," Iris answered sarcastically.

"No need for that tone," cautioned her father, and Iris sighed.

"Okay," she said. "Sorry."

Then they just ate for a while, and the only conversation was the clink of their glasses against the wooden tabletop and the scrape of their forks against the ceramic plates.

In the relative silence, Iris heard something from the front hallway. A kind of rasping, scratchy sound. She wondered if it came from the closet under the stairs. It sounded like it came from the closet under the stairs.

She put down her fork and listened carefully, waiting to see if the sound would come again. It did.

"Did you hear that?"

"What?" asked her dad loudly.

"Shhh." Iris strained to hear. There it was again. "That."

"We probably have mice," said her mom. "This is an old place."

"If Charles were a *real* cat," said her dad, "he'd take care of that for us."

But Iris didn't think the sound was from a mouse.

After dinner, Iris and her parents washed the dishes. They had to do it by hand because there wasn't a dishwasher. They had an assembly line: her dad washed, her mom dried, and Iris put away.

It didn't take very long, but even so, Iris resented the lack of modern kitchen appliances. The farmhouse was over one hundred years old, and apparently no one who had lived in it during the last half century had thought it worthwhile to bring a few things up to date.

"I think it's charming," her mother said when Iris complained about it.

"That's because you're drying instead of washing," said her dad, scrubbing at the stubborn lasagna tray. "We're getting a dishwasher."

Iris felt a surge of triumph, like she'd won a point against the old farmhouse. *Fifteen–Love,* she thought, keeping score, out of habit, like she would a tennis match.

As soon as she thought the words, she regretted them. Thinking about tennis made her think about Sarah.

Iris's mom had played doubles tennis all through high school and college. She had been a star — her height, her long arms, and her broad shoulders all combined into one heck of a mean serve. So she'd loved it when Sarah would spend the weekend at their house and the four of them — Sarah, Iris, her mom and dad — would walk over to the local high school to play together. Iris and her dad weren't great, but they did their best to keep up — the grownups on one side of the net, Iris and Sarah on the other. But most of the matches ended up coming down to Sarah and Iris's mom, with Iris and her dad just standing there, rackets in hand. Iris was built like her dad—like one of the fairy folk, he liked to joke. He wore smaller shoes than his wife did.

Every time Sarah scored a point, she'd trill out a chirp of joy, like it was the first time she'd ever done such a thing. Like she'd surprised herself. Then she'd call out the score, gleeful—"Fifteen–Love," or "Thirty–Fifteen," or whatever. Scoring tennis was funny; both sides started out with "Love," which equaled nothing. The first and second points were each worth fifteen; the third point was worth ten. The first side to get a fourth point won— as long as the opposing side was at least two points behind. If not, scoring got even more complicated. Iris hated keeping score, so it was always Sarah's job.

Before every serve, Sarah would spin the racket in her hands, tapping the head and loosening her grip on the handle so it'd spin around and around. She always did it three times—never twice, never four times. Iris teased her about it, but she had her own tennis habit too—rocking back onto her heels and then up onto her toes, once for each time Sarah's tennis racket spun.

And Sarah double-knotted her laces before every match, pulling them so tight that sometimes later she couldn't get them undone and had to ask Iris's dad for help.

Afterward they'd get ice cream if it was summer, or fluffy warm drinks from the coffee shop if it was winter. There had never been a day when they'd had to skip a game on account of rain. When they lost, Sarah was always gracious about it, but when they won, she couldn't help but gloat and rub it in. Together like that, with her parents and Sarah, Iris had felt comfortably, unremarkably content.

Sarah's racket leaned against the wall inside the hall closet. Sarah's parents had given it to Iris when she had been packing to leave town.

"It's a good racket," Sarah's mom had said tearfully. "And Sarah wouldn't have wanted it to go to anyone else."

Corvallis weather was not tennis-friendly. Iris hadn't touched the racket once since her dad had set it in the closet under the stairs. Not that Iris felt like playing, anyway.

They watched a movie in the living room after they finished in the kitchen. Iris's dad built the fire up higher, and Iris sat wedged between her parents on the couch. They'd all changed into flannel pajamas, and their feet, lined up together on the leather ottoman, looked like a set in gray wool socks.

Charles was purring at last, curled up like a skin ball on Iris's mom's stomach. Iris's eyes didn't stay on the screen. Instead she focused on the fire, watching the flickering yellow and orange, the glowing log that collapsed, finally, throwing off a shower of sparks amid a burst of crackles.

It was cozy. Iris didn't like to admit it, but there were some okay things about their new house. Their new life.

But then Iris glanced at her mom's face. She wasn't watching the movie, either. She looked lost, and her face looked older, in a way that scared Iris.

Her mother must have felt Iris looking at her. She snapped out of her reverie and turned to Iris, smiling. "Hey there, Pigeon," she said.

Iris smiled back. "Coo," she answered.

Iris loved that her parents called her Pigeon. They had called her Pigeon as long as Iris could remember. The story was that when Iris was a baby, her happy gurgling noises sounded just like a pigeon's.

They watched the movie after that, and eventually Iris felt tiny little weights pulling at her eyelids. The next thing she knew she was pressed into her father's chest, his unshaven chin brushing her forehead as he carried her upstairs. She pretended to still be asleep as her mother pulled back her covers, as her father laid her down, as they tucked the blankets up around her shoulders, as they kissed her cheek—first the soft, fragrant touch of her mother, then her father's roughness—and as they left the room.

4

The next day at lunch, Boris told Iris, "I have something for you." Then he pried open the Velcro on his camouflage-printed reusable lunch bag and extracted an apple.

It was mottled green-pink-red and felt cool in Iris's palm.

"Thank you," she said.

"It's a Pink Lady," Boris added, his level of enthusiasm way too high for an apple, Iris thought. But he looked at her so expectantly that she bit in.

Sweet-tart juice squirted into her mouth. Her eyes widened. She took another bite. Then another.

"Wow," she said at last. "This really is good."

Boris nodded, as proud as if he had farmed the apple himself. "I told you so."

After that, Iris decided that it might not be completely terrible to be sort-of friends with Boris. It would make her mother happy, she reasoned, for her to have a friend. And it would be easier to hang out with Boris than to go through all the trouble of getting to know someone else. The girls all seemed nice enough, but none of them brought her an apple or anything, and the thought of getting close with any of them . . . well, it wasn't appealing, that was for sure.

So being friends with Boris was one good thing. And the new routine of switching classes every hour—the ringing of bells, the four-minute rush in the hallway between periods, the different desks, each with something carved into its surface, and having six teachers instead of one—those were good things too.

It took less than a month for Iris to learn everything she thought there was to know about Boris: he was a die-hard Magic player. He thought Minecraft was way cooler than Cubelands. He had four siblings, all sisters—two older and two younger. The oldest was Margaret. She was away at college in Eugene. The next oldest, Eileen, was a junior in high school. His younger sisters were twins—Molly and Charlotte. They were nine.

Because he was the only boy in his family, Boris had his own room, while his sisters had to share. Since Margaret had left for college, Eileen had a room to herself, too, during the week, but Margaret came home most weekends—"to get home-cooked meals and make our mom do her laundry. And to visit her loser boyfriend, Steve. Well, Dad says he's a loser. I think he's okay because he lets me use his employee discount at Max's Cavalcade of Comics, where he works. I just got a Liliana of the Veil last weekend."

Iris didn't ask what a Liliana of the Veil was. But of course Boris told her anyway.

"Liliana is this incredibly amazing Magic card. She's a Mythic Rare. I saw one for sale on eBay for twenty-five dollars. And the auction was still going on! I got mine for seventeen fifty."

Iris's house was the bus driver's first stop in the mornings, and before long, Iris started saving a seat for Boris.

Once a girl named Heather tried to sit down next to her, before Boris's stop. Her hair was light red, like Sarah's hair, but curly instead of straight. She had a nice smile and wore interesting socks—argyle one day, plaid the next—but Iris put her hand across the bench and told her that the seat was saved.

Of course some of the stupid kids decided that Iris and Boris sitting on the bus together and sharing a table at lunch meant that they were girlfriend and boyfriend, and Iris pretended that it didn't embarrass her when they made kissy noises as Boris slid onto the seat next to her.

Boris seemed oblivious most of the time, but once, when one of the big eighth-graders, the boy who scored the most points at lunchtime basketball, announced, "The fat kid's got a girlfriend! I guess miracles really can happen, huh?" she saw Boris's brow furrow in a way that showed how he really felt.

Neither Boris nor Iris spoke about the incident, seeming to tacitly agree that the best way to handle stupid people was to pretend they didn't exist. She wondered who Boris had sat next to before she moved to town, but didn't ask. If Sarah had been there, things would have been different. She never let people get away with that sort of stuff. At home, whenever Iris pointed out stuff like that, Sarah had known what to do.

Iris remembered something Sarah used to say, about Iris's name—how an iris is the name of a flower, but also a part of the eye. She used to say that Iris was sweet like a flower, but a "seer," too, someone who noticed things that might not be obvious to everyone else.

Iris had loved that, the idea that just by noticing what was around her, she was doing something maybe important. She'd point things out to Sarah, and Sarah would act.

But without Sarah, Iris didn't know what to do with the things she noticed—the way so many of the kids mocked Boris, the way he pretended not to care but really, Iris knew, he did.

Back home, with Sarah, Iris felt that she had been better in every way. More complete. With Sarah, she had been balanced and whole. Here, far from home and from Sarah, amid all the rain and all these strangers, Iris felt . . . halved.

She and Boris had most of their classes in common, though Boris was in a more advanced math and Iris was a year ahead in Spanish.

Most of the time Iris could float along, minding her own business. But the girls from the first day on the bus—the heart drawers—were in her Spanish class, too. Starla and Isobel.

And, watching Starla and Isobel's steps fall in unison as they headed together out of class when the bell screamed the end of the period, Iris felt a sharp tearing inside, of sadness and envy, too.

A few times, Boris invited her to visit his house, but Iris always made up an excuse, until one day when her dad drove to Portland for some special gardening supplies and her mom needed to stay late at the university to do something with a culture she was growing in her lab.

Her parents said she could go home by herself if she wanted, or she could walk over to her mom's office and wait there, but neither of these options sounded very appealing to Iris.

"Hey, Boris," she said at lunch. "Can I come to your place this afternoon?"

Boris grinned.

Iris borrowed Boris's cell phone to call her mom and pretended not to hear the surprise in her mother's voice when she said where she was going. She promised to call again from Boris's house and got off the phone as quickly as possible, hoping no one else on the bus had been listening to the conversation. At Boris's stop, Iris climbed out along with the mass of kids who all lived in his housing tract.

Walking down the street toward Boris's house, the hood of her rain slicker pulled up over her head, Iris looked at all the houses. They really were like a wetter version of the houses in her old neighborhood in Seal Beach. But things seemed looser here, messier. Lawns were overgrown and wild, not edged around the driveways and walkways. Bicycles lay slanted across front porches; helmets sat beside them like flipped-over turtles. The cars here were older, too, some rimmed with rust, many with bumper stickers that Iris didn't really understand but that seemed vaguely political.

Back home in Seal Beach, the houses in her neighborhood had been packed close together like these, maybe even closer, but she'd never really noticed. Probably it was living out at the old farmhouse—her dad had started calling it "the homestead"—that made her see how these houses were all so alike, and how narrow their yards were.

Boris led the way, staying half a pace ahead of Iris. When they got to his house, Boris stopped abruptly before turning up the walkway. Iris almost bumped into him.

"Here we are," he said.

"Yep," Iris answered.

Boris's house had a tired-looking minivan parked in its driveway and a gray-blue front door, which he shoved open unceremoniously before dumping his backpack on the bench in the hallway. He kicked his boots underneath it, so Iris did the same.

The entry hall was jam-packed with kid paraphernalia, almost all girl stuff—pink and purple rain slickers doubled up on the hooks above the bench, sneakers with sparkly laces and Crocs with iridescent butterfly charms, and sweaters and sweatshirts in a rainbow of colors.

After taking off her boots, Iris started following Boris toward the kitchen, where she could hear girl voices. Halfway there she stepped on something sharp and cried out.

Boris turned back and watched as Iris hopped on one foot, rubbing the other. He picked up something small and green from the floor.

"Lego brick," he announced solemnly. "Here's a question—what's the plural of Lego?"

Iris felt distinctly annoyed. She was beginning to wonder if maybe she should have gone to her mother's office rather than here.

Boris mistook her silence for interest and answered his own question. "It's funny," he said. "People fight about it all the time on the Internet. Some people say that the plural of Lego is Legos, and some say that the plural is just Lego. You know . . . like the plural of buffalo is buffalo, not buffalos?"

Iris's foot felt better. She stood straight and crossed her arms, waiting for Boris to finish. She'd learned that when Boris got really revved up, it was best to just let him get whatever he was talking about out of his system.

"But really," he said, laughing a little, "they're *both*

wrong. Lego is the name of the company, not the individual pieces. The pieces should really be called Lego bricks, not Lego or Legos. But no one wants to hear *that* little piece of information."

Including me, thought Iris, but instead she said, "I'm hungry. Do you have any snacks?"

One thing that Boris could always be counted on for was good snacks. He brought all kinds of stuff to share at lunch, and once she was in his kitchen, Iris could see why.

His two younger sisters were sitting at a round white table, digging into a bowl of cut-up fruit, dipping the pieces into melted chocolate. Behind them on the kitchen's longest wall was an enormous cabinet with glass-fronted doors completely packed with colorful containers, each bearing a neatly printed label: CHEERIOS. FRUIT ROLLS. BEEF JERKY. TURKEY JERKY. SALMON JERKY. GOLDFISH. DRIED FRUIT. ALMONDS. WALNUTS. PISTACHIOS.

"Have whatever you want," Boris said. He took out a couple of the nut containers and shook their contents into a bowl, then he grabbed the container marked CHOCOLATE CHIPS and poured a bunch of those in too.

"Who's that?" one of the twins asked.

"This is Iris," Boris said begrudgingly. "Iris, those are the twins."

A more obvious statement had never been made, Iris thought. The girls were identical down to the ribbons in their hair—light blue velvet. They had Boris's same brown curly hair and thick short bodies. They wore red and white striped tights under blue corduroy jumpers and red turtleneck sweaters.

"Is she your girlfriend?" the other twin asked.

"Gross," said Boris, and Iris was glad to hear her own thoughts voiced out loud.

"You're the first friend Boris has brought home in years," one of the twins said.

"Years," said the other.

Boris looked half angry, half embarrassed. Iris wasn't sure if she was supposed to respond.

The first twin dipped the last apple slice into the bowl of chocolate before sliding down from her chair. "C'mon, Char," she said. *"Dance School Dropout* is about to start."

"The twins are addicted to reality television," Boris told Iris.

"At least we're not addicted to stupid computer

games," Molly shot back, and Charlotte cackled like that was the funniest insult she'd ever heard.

Boris settled in with his snack, and Iris poured herself some cereal. It took her a minute to find the refrigerator; its doors were surfaced with the same white paneling as the row of cabinets that surrounded it. "Cool," she said when she found the handle and pulled it open.

She poured milk over her cereal. Boris took one look at the jug and shook his head. "Two percent," he said.

They ate their snacks. When they were almost done, Boris said, "Is it weird for you to be here? You know, at a friend's house?"

Iris had told him the week before that her best friend back home had died. She had the feeling that Boris already knew, like maybe his parents had told him or something, and she didn't want it hanging out there like some big untouchable secret, though she didn't want to talk about it either. She hadn't offered any details, and she was glad that Boris hadn't asked for them.

"No," said Iris. She almost said, "Is it weird for *you* to have a friend over?" but decided at the last minute that she didn't really want to be mean.

But she also didn't want to talk about Sarah. Not with Boris.

Or her parents, though they kept trying. When Iris had asked them what they thought about ghosts—just in general, nothing specific, they had given each other worried looks and started talking about the counselor they thought Iris should maybe visit. Dr. Shannon.

Iris didn't like the sound of that at all. She'd had to go to a psychiatrist a few times already, right after Sarah's death. He'd given her a bunch of dolls and encouraged her to do whatever she wanted with them. She just lined them all up side by side as he nodded and studied them like what she'd done had some deep meaning.

Then he'd given her some paper and asked her to draw a picture of her favorite people, and when she'd drawn three stick figures—a tall one for her mom, a medium-size one for her dad, and a cat-shaped one for Charles, he'd asked, "Why did you only draw three?"

This seemed like a completely stupid question to Iris, who answered, "Because Sarah is dead. You know that, right?"

Not very long after that, her parents announced that they had found a buyer for the house and that the three of them were moving to Oregon. One of the move's redeeming characteristics was that it had put an end to the visits with the psychiatrist, and Iris had figured that was that. But apparently her mom and dad had different plans.

Probably talking about ghosts wasn't the best way to discourage future visits to mental health care professionals. But Iris couldn't shake the feeling that there *was* a ghost—her best friend's ghost—living at the farmhouse with them.

Not living. That was the wrong word, of course. Ghosts don't live. That was the whole point. So . . . what? Existing? Floating?

Whatever the right verb was, Iris felt sure of the facts. Sarah was there. At the homestead. In the closet under the stairs.

5

Boris's mom came into the kitchen while Iris and Boris were still eating their snack. Iris liked her right away. For one thing, she introduced herself as Katherine rather than Mrs. McBride. Iris didn't like it when adults wanted kids to call them by their last names. It didn't seem democratic.

Katherine also didn't ask them if they wanted hot chocolate; she just went ahead and made a big batch, stirring it in a pot on the stove rather than microwaving it cup by cup. And there was whipped cream in the refrigerator, which she didn't hold back on.

"Thank you," Iris said when Katherine handed her a

large, hot mug. The mug had a picture of a fluffy orange kitten curled up in a hammock with the word *Catnap!* underneath.

"Sip carefully," Katherine warned. "It's hot."

She gave Boris a cup too and put two more on a tray for the twins.

"Where's Eileen?" Iris asked Boris.

He shrugged. "Probably at a friend's," he said. "C'mon. I want to show you my Magic collection."

It was clear from Boris's room that he had lived in the same house since he was born. It would take at least a dozen years to collect that much *stuff*.

His room was as neatly organized as the kitchen pantry. He had a four-poster single bed. On top of each post was a carved pineapple. There was a desk that was made out of the same kind of wood as the bed, and the top of it was entirely cleared off except for a closed black laptop and a brass lamp. The bookshelf across from the bed held a few toys—a Rubik's Cube, a dragon statuette, an old stuffed elephant—and neat rows of books. Boris slid open the closet door to reveal stacked bins marked LEGO BRICKS, WOODEN BLOCKS, LINCOLN LOGS, CHEMISTRY STUFF,

MAGNETS, MISCELLANEOUS PARTS, and ACTION FIGURES. And far to one side were three tall boxes marked identically— MAGIC CARDS.

Iris sighed and spun around in the chair by Boris's desk. This was going to take a while, she could tell, so she made herself comfortable and sipped her chocolate.

Boris launched into an enthusiastic lecture about all things Magic, and Iris did her best to look interested. This got a lot harder after she'd finished her hot chocolate and there was nothing to preoccupy her. It was growing more and more clear why it had been so long since Boris had had a guest.

Finally Boris said, "I'll tell you what I'm going to do. I'm going to build you a starter deck so that you can get a feel for the game. I'll teach you how to play. You can be, like, my Padawan."

"Uh-huh," said Iris. "Sure. That sounds great."

It actually sounded the opposite of great.

But being in Boris's room *felt* almost great, which surprised Iris. The hot chocolate was first-rate, and at least there was plenty to do over here. Maybe learning to play Magic would be a small price to pay.

"So if you don't have a lot of friends over," she asked, trying to be nice, "who do you play Magic with?"

"My dad, mostly. Sometimes this kid Bradley up the street, but he's only eight and kind of a geek."

Don't laugh, don't laugh, don't laugh, Iris ordered herself.

Then she remembered that she was supposed to call her mom. "Hey," she asked, "can I use your phone?"

Boris was absorbed in his cards, quickly sorting through stacks of them and occasionally setting one to the side. "It's in the kitchen," he said, without looking up.

On her way back to the kitchen, Iris poked her head into each of the open doorways she passed. The room right next to Boris's was clearly the twins'; it was divided down the center by a strip of blue masking tape—across the floor and back up the wall on the far side. Stepping into the room, Iris looked behind her at the doorway. The blue line of tape ended at the white molding that framed the door, and Iris wondered if each twin was careful to use only her own half of the entrance.

Based on how the girls dressed, Iris would have guessed that their tastes would be identical in every way.

But she would have been wrong. One slice of the room was as neat as Boris's, and the other was practically a masterpiece of filth. Unmade bed, socks and pajama bottoms everywhere, books and toys and hair ribbons all sloshed together on the bed and spilling onto the ground. Not one object, though, crossed that blue line on the floor. It was like the stuff knew better than to try.

The next room was a bathroom, with all the usual towels and scrunched-up toothpaste tubes. Across the hall was Margaret and Eileen's room. It had twin beds too, and again the room was clearly divided by its occupants. Eileen's side had a stack of schoolbooks on its desk and two pairs of boots strewn on the floor near the bed. Margaret's side looked more clinical. Not so lived-in. Like its occupant was dead.

Iris knew that Boris's sister Margaret wasn't dead. She was away at college. She told herself to stop being morbid and moved on.

There was one more room at the end of the hallway, in the opposite direction of the kitchen. Iris decided that it must belong to Boris's parents, and she didn't want to get caught snooping there, though she was curious what it might look like.

Instead, she headed the other way. She could see the twins on the floor in front of the TV; their empty hot chocolate cups sat on an end table as they stared, transfixed, at what must have been *Dance School Dropout*. A skinny girl in a pink tutu sat crying on a wooden floor. Two other girls, in identical skirts, stared down at her with their arms folded across their chests.

In the kitchen, Iris found Katherine at the round white table, sipping a cup of tea and reading a novel.

"Excuse me?"

Katherine blinked and looked up. "Need more hot chocolate?"

"Umm . . . no . . . I mean, yeah, more hot chocolate would be great . . . but I was wondering if I could use your phone? To call my mom?"

"Of course." Katherine gestured to the wall near the stove, where a phone was hanging.

Iris had never seen a phone like this in an actual house before, only in old movies. It wasn't wireless; a long, tightly curled cord connected the red plastic receiver to the base, where twelve buttons in a little square were marked with numbers, an asterisk, and a hashtag.

"Can you get online with this phone?" Iris asked.

"Nope," Katherine said. "All that phone does is make calls."

"Then what's that for?" Iris pointed to the hashtag. "Isn't that for Twitter?"

Katherine laughed. "It's a whole new world," she said, more to herself than to Iris.

Iris picked up the handle and punched in her mom's work number.

Her mom answered in her business voice. "Dr. Abernathy here."

"Hi, Mom, it's me."

"Iris, *there* you are!"

"I'm at Boris's house."

"Can I talk to his mother?" she said.

"Mm-hmm," said Iris. "Just a minute."

She held the phone out to Katherine. "My mom wants to talk to you."

Katherine put down her book and reached for the receiver. The cord stretched straighter as Iris passed it across the table.

"Hello, this is Boris's mom, Katherine."

Iris couldn't hear all her mother's words, but she heard the murmur of her voice. The up-and-down of it.

"It's my pleasure," said Katherine. "Iris is welcome anytime."

They talked for a couple of minutes more—Katherine asked Iris's mom how she was enjoying life in Corvallis, and what her specialty was at the university.

Iris waited as her mom responded, picking out words here and there like "infectious disease research" and "lots of rain," and then she heard the upturn of her mother's muffled voice, as if she'd asked a question.

"American Dream is the best pizza joint in town," Katherine said. She sounded almost as enthusiastic as Boris had about Magic.

Finally they hung up. Katherine rose to replace the receiver, then mixed more chocolate and milk in a pot, lighting the burner and stirring until the chocolate steamed. Iris went back to Boris's room to get her *Catnap!* mug. Boris was sorting through a stack of cards with a satisfied expression on his face.

"You want another cup of hot chocolate?" Iris asked.

"Huh?" Boris looked up. "Oh. No, thanks. I still haven't finished mine."

Iris scooped up her cup and took it back to the kitchen.

"Do you have any more whipped cream?" she asked after Katherine filled her cup with hot chocolate.

"A woman after my own heart," said Katherine, pulling the red and white canister from the door of the fridge.

Iris was pretty sure that a game of Magic was waiting for her back in Boris's room, so she slid into one of the kitchen chairs. "What are you reading?"

"Just a silly novel about a silly woman," Katherine said. "I don't get much time for pleasure reading, so I'm not sure I'll finish it."

Iris nodded, even though she'd never started a book that she hadn't finished. She sipped her cocoa and tried to think of an interesting question to ask.

"Have you always lived here?" Not thrilling, but a start.

Katherine shook her head. "I moved every three years growing up," she said. "My dad was in the military. But I decided that when I had kids, I'd make sure they had a stable life. So we've been in this house since just a few months after our first daughter was born."

Iris licked away her whipped-cream mustache. "That's nice," she said.

Katherine's expression changed, like she had just remembered that Iris had been recently uprooted, like maybe she knew why. "Of course, moving can be great, too," she added. "A fresh start."

Hearing the echo of her parents' new favorite phrase made Iris lose her taste for the sweet drink, and she set her cup back onto the table.

"I guess," she said. She thought about going back to Boris's room, but before she did, she said, "You know, even if you try to give your kids a really stable life, sometimes things happen that aren't part of your plan."

Katherine nodded. "That's the truth," she said. "Has Boris told you his birth story?"

Iris shook her head, a little embarrassed to have the image of Boris being born spring to her mind.

"You should ask him about it. Talk about things not going the way you expect." She sipped her tea. After a minute she said, "Boris is my miracle."

Iris could have laughed, but the tone of Katherine's voice stopped her. She sounded completely sincere.

Katherine said, "Well, all children are miracles. But some are more miraculous than others."

Iris didn't know what to say to this, so she stood up. "I think Boris wants to teach me how to play Magic," she said. "Thanks for the cocoa."

"Anytime, sweetie." Katherine turned back to her book.

Boris spent the next hour and a half explaining the intricacies of Magic. Iris did her best to be a good guest and pay attention, but by the time her mom arrived to pick her up, Iris's left eye was twitching.

She heard the doorbell and sprang up, scattering the cards in front of her.

"Sorry," she said. "I've gotta go. Thanks for having me over."

"Here!" Boris stacked up the deck Iris had been using and wrapped it with a rubber band from his desk drawer. "Take these with you. They're for you to keep. Bring them to school and we can play at lunch if you want."

Iris couldn't think of a polite way to refuse.

She found her mom talking with Katherine just inside the front door. Their expressions were serious, and when her mom caught sight of Iris, she seemed to quickly change the subject.

This wasn't the first time Iris had seen this happen — some caring adult leaning in to listen to Iris's mom, commiserating, maybe, or sympathizing. It had happened more often in Seal Beach — at the grocery store, or the coffee shop, even outside the house by the row of mailboxes. Here in Corvallis not everyone knew their whole story, so Iris was spared most of those looks, those overheard snippets of conversation. But not all of them.

"Thanks again for looking after Iris," her mom said.

"Yeah, thanks, Katherine," Iris said as she pulled on her boots and raincoat.

"Did you have a nice time?" asked Katherine.

Iris silently weighed the hot chocolate against the compulsory game of Magic, but finally nodded.

"Come back anytime." Katherine switched on the porch light and waved after them as Iris and her mom made a run for the car through the rain. The day had dimmed to evening, and Iris saw the puffs of her breath as she splashed down the walkway.

Then they slammed themselves into the car, her mom cranked on the heat to high, and they headed home.

6

When Iris and her mom got home, Iris couldn't help but compare Boris's house to the "homestead."

Boris's house had other kids. Fifteen–Love.

Boris's house had an endless supply of snacks. Thirty–Love.

Boris's house didn't feel sad. Forty–Love.

"Meow," said Charles. He stood by the cold, dark fireplace, as if imploring Iris to do something about it.

The homestead had Charles. Maybe that was something.

"Mom," Iris called, "Charles wants a fire."

"So build him one," her mom called back. "Let me know if you want help lighting it."

Iris had never built a fire before. She'd ask her dad for help, but he still wasn't back from Portland. Charles looked desperate. Well, how hard could it be to build a fire?

There were logs stacked next to the fireplace. Iris pulled open the screen and piled a few pieces on the grate, trying to leave room in between for air.

She rummaged through her father's stack of newspapers, checking to make sure each crossword puzzle she came across was completely filled in before crumpling the sheet and stuffing it between the logs.

On the mantel was the long-nosed lighter. It seemed kind of silly to call her mother in just to ignite the newspapers, so Iris pushed down the safety latch and pulled the lighter's trigger.

A tiny orange flame sprang to life. Charles stepped forward and twitched his nose. He looked happier already.

Iris touched the flame to one exposed newspaper edge. It blackened, wrinkled back a little, then glowed hot as it caught fire. Charles leaped up onto the hearth, settled next to Iris, and curled his tail around his legs.

Iris and Charles watched as the fire grew. His ears were forward, like he was trying to warm the tips of them.

Iris held her hands out too, rubbing them in front of the growing flames.

Almost as good as the light and warmth, Iris thought, *is a fire's sound.* She listened to the wood as it shifted and crackled. Like it was another voice. Next to her, Charles relaxed, his tail unfurling as the room warmed.

Then there was the sound of tires on gravel, followed by the slam of a car door. A moment later the front door swung open and banged closed. Iris's dad was home.

"Hello, hello," he called. Iris heard two thumps as his boots dropped onto the rubber mat he had placed near the door. Then he came into the den.

"Pigeon!" he said. "Did you build that fire all by yourself?"

"Uh-huh."

Her dad came over and examined her handiwork. "Lots of room for air," he said. "Just enough newspaper. Crossword puzzles?"

"Only the filled-in ones."

"That's my girl." He rubbed her hair affectionately. Iris blew the strands out of her face. "You sure are getting grown up. What else can you do that I don't know about?"

Iris shrugged.

"What did you do this afternoon?"

Iris told her dad about visiting Boris's house. She told him about Magic and the incredible assortment of snack food. Then she asked him about Portland and the special gardening store he'd visited.

His eyes twinkled in a way that Iris hadn't seen in a long time. At first she thought that maybe it was just the firelight, but as he told her all about his trip to the city—"You should have seen this place, Pigeon! So many different kinds of organic fertilizers!"—Iris slowly realized that the shine in her father's expression was because he was happy.

And she realized that this made her mad. It didn't seem right that he would be happy—*could* be happy—just six months after Sarah's death.

She remembered how he had looked—how both of her parents had looked—in the weeks after that terrible day. How would they have looked if she had been standing slightly to the left, in Sarah's place? If the outcome were different? If Sarah were alive, and maybe Iris were dead instead?

* * *

At dinner, her dad told them all about his plans for spring. "I really think that I can grow most of our food right here on our own land! It'll take a few seasons, but I think we can be pretty autonomous. And guess what else . . ." He looked like he could barely contain his surprise. "Chickens!" he burst out at last. "We're getting chickens! Chicks in the spring—we can hatch them ourselves, in a rented incubator from the shop in Portland."

"For eggs, right? The chickens will lay eggs?"

Her father, who had been alternately digging into his dinner and gesturing with both his fork and knife, turned to Iris. "Sure," he said. "Some of them."

Iris wasn't hungry anymore. "What about the rest of them?"

Iris's mother cleared her throat.

Her dad didn't notice. "Well, sweetie," he said, "they won't all be hens. Some of them will be egg layers, and some of them will be fryers."

"For *frying?*"

"We buy chicken all the time at the store," he said. "This will just be . . . cutting out the middleman."

"No way." Iris's voice was shaking, but not quiet. "There is *no way* we are killing chickens."

Iris's dad opened his mouth to respond, but her mom gave him one of her *looks*. He closed his mouth. After a moment he said, "Okay. No fryers."

"No fryers," Iris repeated. Then she said, "May I be excused?"

U pstairs, her room was cold, which didn't make a lot of sense to Iris because she thought that heat was supposed to rise.

She flopped onto her bed and stared at the ceiling. She thought about her father, how excited he had looked. She thought about chickens. Fryers and layers. After a while she got up and pulled the deck of Magic cards out of her backpack. She returned to her bed and shuffled the cards for a while, liking the sound they made when she split the deck, arched the cards, and fanned them back together. Apart, together. Apart, together. She liked that—how you could take a deck of cards and divide it into pieces and then put it together again, in a completely different order, but that it was still the same deck.

As long as all the cards were there, she reminded herself. If you lose just one card, then all you have is a bunch of laminated rectangular pieces of paper. It's not really a deck anymore at all. She supposed that this wasn't exactly true with Magic cards. In that game, you *could* switch out one card for another. But, Iris thought, that would feel traitorous.

I ris woke up briefly when her parents came in to check on her later. The cards had spilled from her hands all over the bedspread and onto the floor, and Iris heard herself say, "Make sure they're all there. All sixty of them," and she felt her mom pull off her socks while her dad turned back the covers and tucked her in.

She had no idea what time it was when she woke again, and she wasn't sure what woke her. It wasn't the sound of rain against the roof, which had turned into a downpour. She was certain of it. Whatever it was came from beneath her, not above.

Iris swung up to sitting. She sat very still on the edge of her bed, waiting for the sound to come again.

It didn't.

She knew she should lie down and go back to sleep. Instead, Iris lowered her feet to the cold, wooden-planked floor and felt her way across the room. She pulled her fleece robe from its hook on the back of the door and cinched the belt before running her hand along the wall, finding the light switch and flipping it on, squeezing her eyes tightly at first and then slowly opening them, just a crack, then a little more, until at last she could open them all the way.

Her room all around her looked perfectly average—the boxes still stacked in the corners because she hadn't bothered to unpack yet and wouldn't let her dad do it for her, the crumpled clothes in the hamper next to her dresser, a messy desk underneath the night-black window.

Immediately upon leaving her room, Iris regretted letting her eyes adjust to the light. She blinked into the hallway's darkness and felt her way to the banister, then down the steep staircase. There were seventeen stairs. She counted them every time.

On the sixteenth stair, Iris stopped and listened. At last she heard the sound again—it was a lament, a wail, a beseeching prayer.

It came, she thought, from the closet under the stairs.

She stepped down the final stair.

Her eyes were readjusting to the dark. She couldn't see perfectly, but she could make out the six separate panels of the closet door. The knob. The thin, horizontal strip of darkness where the door didn't quite meet the floor.

"Sarah?" she whispered.

Nothing.

Iris imagined what was behind the door—the tennis racket, the rod of hangers each holding a body-shaped coat, the basket of gloves and hats.

"Sarah," she said again. "Are you there?"

She heard another sound. The hairs on the back of her neck stood straight. Her heart either pounded harder or missed a beat—she couldn't tell which. Her stomach roiled with fear.

All children are miracles, Katherine had said.

And though her family wasn't religious, Iris closed her eyes and prayed. *Give me a miracle.*

Then she opened the closet door.

The coats on the rack swung gently, though there was no draft.

Iris blinked back tears. "Sarah?"

It wasn't Sarah; not this time. The coats parted and the cat emerged from the shadows.

"Charles," Iris said.

His *meow* was pitiful. He shivered and rubbed against Iris's leg.

Iris picked him up and tucked him into her robe. He started purring immediately, like he was too relieved to worry about conserving energy. Iris gently shut the closet door and went back upstairs. When she got to her room, she left her robe on and pulled the covers up around her and Charles both. He slept there, against her chest, an oversize heart outside her body.

At breakfast, Iris's mom said, "Did you have a hard time sleeping last night, Pigeon?"

Iris looked up from her plate of eggs and toast. "Sort of. Why?"

Her mom smiled, but it was sad. "I thought maybe I heard you downstairs, saying Sarah's name."

Iris looked back down. She pierced a piece of egg with her fork but didn't eat it.

"We all miss Sarah," said her mom. "Your dad and I miss her too."

A tear slipped from Iris's eye and splashed on her plate.

"Do you want to talk about it?"

Iris shook her head.

"We all *need* to talk about it, baby." Her mom took a sip of coffee. Iris loved to fix her mother's coffee—she loved to scoop in the sugar, pour in the white cream. Her mom liked to keep her spoon in her mug, tucking it behind her index finger to keep it from slipping around and hitting her face.

It would have been simpler to take out the spoon, but her mom liked it that way, so Iris always left the spoon in the cup when she fixed her mom's coffee.

Iris spoke. "I don't know if Sarah is really gone," she said. "Or, at least, not all-the-way gone." It wasn't easy to speak around the lump in her throat, and she had to wait a long time before her mom answered.

"The people we love never go away completely. We keep them with us, in our hearts."

Iris met her mother's eyes and wondered if she really believed that, or if it was just something to say. "I think Sarah is *here*," she said. "I hear her sometimes, moving around."

Her mother nodded, like she wasn't surprised that Iris

had said this, but her face didn't exactly light up with excitement, either. "I think that's probably pretty normal, to hope for that," she said.

Iris felt angry. "Miracles happen, you know."

Her mother took another sip of coffee, the spoon tucked behind her finger. "Do they?"

Iris didn't feel like talking about it anymore. "The bus'll be here soon. I've got to walk down the driveway." She pushed back from the table and went to get her boots and coat from the hallway. Her mother followed her.

"I'm going to make an appointment for us," her mom said. "With Dr. Shannon, in town. We'll all go together, okay?"

Iris didn't answer. She snapped her coat shut and swung her pack onto her back.

"I love you, Pigeon," her mom called after her as she headed out into the rain.

For a second Iris didn't answer. But then she stopped and turned. The rain splashed all around her. "Coo," she called, and lifted her hand in a wave.

She should go about this scientifically, Iris decided. And she should start by doing the necessary research.

Boris had a thermos full of split-pea soup and a roll of round butter crackers. He dipped the crackers into the soup and nibbled at them, raining down soupy crumbs onto the table. He hadn't bothered packing a spoon. Iris considered telling him that maybe it was habits such as this that made cultivating friendships difficult for him, but she didn't want to get into a whole conversation about it, so she just sat down across from him and opened her bag. Her dad had picked up a reusable lunch bag for her at the co-op, and he even wrapped her sandwich now in a rectangle of plastic-lined cloth that buttoned closed. Her juice was in a reusable PBA-free plastic bottle. Her lunch looked just like all the other Corvallis lunches.

The lunch inside, however, was undeniably delicious. Since her dad had begun his "conscious rebellion against packaged foods," instead of plastic-wrapped string cheese, he was sending her to school with homemade mozzarella balls. Almost every morning, the warm-wet scent of fresh baked bread filled the kitchen. And there was even talk of purchasing a yogurt maker.

"Boris," she said as she unwrapped her sandwich, "tell me about your miracle."

Boris screwed up his mouth like he'd tasted something sour. "My mom told you about that, huh?"

"She sure did."

"I hate when she does that."

Iris waited a minute to give Boris a chance to process. Then, after he'd eaten two more pea soup–soaked crackers, she prodded him. "Well?"

He groaned. "Do we really have to talk about this? While I'm *eating?*"

Iris nodded. She didn't point out that she had to stomach Boris's lunching habits daily, and whatever he was feeling squeamish about couldn't possibly be that bad.

"It's no big deal," Boris began reluctantly. "Well, I guess it's actually a really big deal. See, I wasn't supposed to live. The doctors told my parents I'd be born dead, or maybe I'd die right after I was born."

"Wow. How come?"

"It's kind of embarrassing."

"I won't laugh. I promise."

He sighed. "It's my urinary tract," he confided. "When I was developing, I couldn't . . . I couldn't pee, all right? And so the doctors thought my kidneys were going to be all messed up, and my bladder ruptured while I was still inside my mom—"

"Ruptured?" interrupted Iris. "You mean like ... it popped?"

Boris nodded. "Uh-huh. And also, the water that surrounded me—the amniotic fluid—it was way too low, which made the doctors worry that my lungs wouldn't develop right, because without enough amniotic fluid, your lungs can't grow. And if that had happened, then when I was born and tried to breathe, my lungs could have just cracked apart and I would have died within a few minutes. And there wasn't anything the doctors could do about it, and pretty much all the babies the doctors had ever heard of who had my problem didn't make it. They all died. So I was supposed to be dead too."

He stopped and dipped another cracker into his soup. Clearly, Iris thought, this story had a happy ending; here he was, alive and well, able to tell his tale and gross her out with his dripping green crackers.

"So what happened?"

"It depends on who you ask. The doctors say I must have spontaneously healed myself. That somehow my kidneys and my bladder got better, even though they couldn't explain why. And also, suddenly there was enough amniotic fluid, even though there hadn't been enough before. Anyway, no one expected me to live. I mean, I had to have a couple of surgeries after I was born, but not big surgeries."

"That's pretty amazing," said Iris. She imagined what that had felt like for Boris's mom and dad—to know that their baby was probably going to die, and that they were helpless to stop it. She thought about how relieved they must have been when he lived. And when he *kept* living, and growing.

"So who says you're a miracle?" she asked. "The doctors?"

"Nah, they just say that I'm really lucky. But my mom's cousin is Catholic—I mean, we're Catholic too, but not like her, we just go to church on Easter and sometimes Midnight Mass before Christmas. My mom's cousin Joanne is *seriously* Catholic. When I was sick and all, before I was born, and Joanne found out about it, she wrote a letter to this group of nuns down in Northern California. Near Berkeley. And those nuns prayed for me. Do you know anything about Catholicism?"

Iris shook her head.

"Well, Catholics, when they pray, they don't always pray directly to God. Sometimes they pray to saints, and sometimes they pray to people they want to *become* saints. Anyway, there was this pope that had died a long time ago, and this group of nuns wanted him to become a saint, so they prayed to him."

"What exactly is a saint?" asked Iris. "Like, a really good person?"

Boris shook his head. "Nah, it's way more complicated than that. See, to be a saint, there are all these steps. First, you have to live, like, a really virtuous life. And then you have to die."

"You have to be dead to be a saint?"

"Uh huh. But there's more. Someone, or some group of people—Catholics, of course—has to want you to become a saint. And that group of people has to prove to the Vatican that you should become a saint."

"Who's the Vatican?"

"Don't you know *anything?*"

Iris had to stop herself from rolling her eyes.

Now Boris was really on fire. "The Vatican is the group of men that's in charge of the Catholic Church. Like, its government. The head guy is the pope. They're all over in Italy."

"Is the pope the president?"

"Sort of. Except that once he's made pope, he doesn't have to be reelected, and he's the pope from then on. Until he dies. At least, that's how it usually goes."

"So what about the miracle?" Lunch was almost over. In a minute the girl with the braids would roll out the bin full of balls.

"Well, this group of nuns wanted this one dead pope to become a saint. And in order for him to become a saint, they'd have to prove that he had performed a miracle. So when my mom was pregnant with me and I was supposed to die, my mom's cousin Joanne told the nuns about me. And they decided to pray to the dead pope to heal me. And when I got better—when I didn't die—they told the Vatican that the pope they prayed to must have cured me."

"But didn't the doctors say that you spontaneously healed?"

Boris shrugged. "That's what the doctors say. The nuns say that their dead pope healed me because they prayed to him."

"Hey, can we move this table?" It was the usual guy, the kid with the really big feet. He wanted to play basketball.

"In a minute," Iris said. "I'm not done with my sandwich yet." She held it up to prove it to him.

He looked annoyed. "Hurry up, lovebirds."

"So what do *you* think?" Iris asked Boris, ignoring the boy's final words. "Was it a miracle, or just really good luck?"

"Honestly? I don't think it matters. I didn't die. That's enough for me."

"But if you should have died . . . if it's a miracle that you lived, and not just really good luck . . . then that means *other* miracles could happen too, right?"

Boris popped the last cracker in his mouth and screwed the lid back onto his thermos. "I guess," he said. "Anyway, the Vatican is still investigating the miracle. There were other miracles, too, that this dead pope was supposedly responsible for. If the Vatican decides they were *real* miracles, and if the living pope signs off on them, then he becomes a saint."

"How do they prove it was really a miracle?"

"My mom had to submit all kinds of paperwork. She

really didn't want to go through the hassle, but her cousin begged her to do it. There was lots of stuff, like my medical records, pictures of me when I was inside my mom, stuff like that. And also, they interviewed the doctors over the phone. And in the spring, they're coming here."

"*Here?* To *Corvallis?*"

Boris nodded. "To talk to my parents and the doctors in person. And to meet me."

Iris thought about that—people coming all the way from Italy just to meet Boris. She wondered if they'd be disappointed when they realized that he was just a normal kid, and that he wasn't even popular or anything. She wondered what it would be like to be in the presence of people like that, people who decided about miracles.

They'd kept their table as long as they could; the big-footed kid didn't ask this time, just jerked his head to indicate that Iris and Boris should get up. They did, and the supervising teacher came over to fold up the table.

"What do you say?" Iris asked, shoving her reusable lunch bag back into her backpack. "Wanna play something?"

"Magic?" Boris's face lit up.

"I was thinking maybe basketball? Or dodge ball?"

"Nah," said Boris. "I don't really like to play any games that involve balls coming at me fast. They make me nervous."

"Huh," said Iris. "That rules out kind of a lot of games."

Boris shrugged. "There aren't any balls in Magic."

This time, Iris couldn't contain her laugh. Boris just stared at her, blinking, waiting for her to finish.

Finally, Iris said, "Sorry. But, you know, don't you ever want to make more friends? You've got to learn to play the games people like if you want to make friends with them."

Boris made a face. "It doesn't seem worth it," he said, walking toward the auditorium door. Iris followed. "I mean, I play their games so that they'll be friends with me, but so what? I won't enjoy myself. Why put myself through all that just to not have fun anyway? I'd rather just be alone. Or with you."

"Well," said Iris, "didn't you get lonely? I mean, before I moved here?"

"Sometimes," Boris admitted. "But I didn't get hurt."

It was *her* room, Iris lamented silently. They were *her* boxes. What business was it of her dad's if she hadn't unpacked yet? Maybe she liked her room like that, with the now-dusty stacks of slightly dented cardboard boxes in both of the far corners.

But he had been insistent, at breakfast, and her mother had been no help.

"The time has come, the walrus said, to speak of many things," her dad had sung as he slid a plate of Iris's favorite—waffles and bacon—in front of her. *"Of shoes and ships and sealing wax, and whether pigs have wings."*

"Why would ceilings need wax?" Iris had asked, playing along as she poured maple syrup on her waffle. She had been in a better-than-usual mood. It was Saturday, she didn't have any homework, and her dad had warmed the syrup.

But he didn't answer. Instead he said, "And time, as well, to speak of your room . . . Do you know, Pigeon, what today is?"

Iris set down the sticky syrup pitcher. Suddenly she suspected that her dad had been softening her up with her favorite breakfast foods.

"No," she answered firmly.

"It's . . . Unpacking Day!" announced her dad, as if this were the best, most exciting news ever.

"No, it's not." Iris looked imploringly at her mom, who was flipping through emails on her phone and sipping her sweetened coffee, the spoon tucked behind her finger.

"Well," said her mom, "let's see . . ." She switched her phone over to its calendar and angled the screen toward Iris. "Hmm . . ." she said. "Look at that. It *is* Unpacking Day."

There, printed in yellow (the color she used for all of Iris's activities and appointments) in the square for November fifth, were the words UNPACKING DAY.

It was a conspiracy.

"You guys just made that up," Iris muttered. "It's not a real thing."

"If the mighty calendar declares it, we mere mortals have no recourse but to do its bidding," said her father in his most regal-sounding voice.

So here she was, sitting cross-legged on her bed, accompanied only by Charles and staring at her boxes, hating them.

Her parents had offered to help, but Iris, of course, refused.

Briefly, Iris considered just carting the boxes into the hallway, kicking them down the stairs, and abandoning them in the rain. After all, she'd lived without all the stuff inside them for the last few months; she probably didn't even need any of it.

But then she remembered that a couple of the boxes held her books, and she didn't want to see them turn into pulpy mush out in the rain, not really, so she sighed and shifted Charles from her lap, tucking him into a blanket before she confronted the first box.

Not books in this one. Shoes, and no wonder she hadn't missed them: the box was full of sandals and flip-flops. Nothing she could wear here. She pulled out one of her favorites, a white leather gladiator sandal with little yellow beads across the toes, and tried it on.

Of course it was too small. She had been on the verge of growing out of this pair before they moved, and now there was no more squeezing into them.

"No reason to empty this one, Charles," Iris told her cat. She tossed the shoe back into the box, carried the whole thing to her door, and set it down in the hallway.

One down. Five to go.

The second and third boxes did contain her books, and Iris spent a happy hour arranging them on the low white bookshelf underneath the window. By the time that was done, she felt a little better.

Then she opened the top box in the second stack and found Sarah staring up at her.

It was a picture—just a picture, of course. But then why did it *feel* that way, like an electric zap? Painful, but proof of life, just the same.

The two of them were in the photo, together. It had been taken last spring, after a round of tennis. Sarah and Iris had won, and in the picture their smiles were triumphant. Sarah was wearing her lucky pink sweatband across her forehead, and Iris's hair was pulled back into two short, uneven braids. Their arms were around each other's shoulders; Iris held her racket up high in triumph, and Sarah rested on hers like a walking stick.

Much of the picture was the wide bright sky behind them, and the chalky green expanse of the tennis court. There was just so *much* of it, Iris thought. So much to miss. And Sarah most of all.

Charles jumped down from the bed and padded out of the room. Then Iris was completely alone. She traced a finger around Sarah's shape. It seemed too much to be-lieve—that *this* could be it, that Sarah had been reduced to photos and possessions. And that even those parts of her had been scattered like leaves, like seeds. This pic-ture and the tennis racket here, in Oregon, and her other things, like her lucky pink sweatband, who knew where those things were . . . ? Maybe Sarah's parents had loaded all that was left of her into boxes—boxes that looked just like these slightly crooked cardboard containers—and had given them away, to charity, to the needy.

I'm the needy, thought Iris, sounding pitiful in her own head. She clasped the picture to her chest and wished, hard, that things could change.

And then Iris suddenly remembered Boris. The Catholic Church believed something had changed for Boris. And if their leaders—the Vatican—believed that a group of nuns had successfully communicated with a dead pope in order to save Boris's life, then maybe it *wasn't* crazy, this feeling Iris had that Sarah was somehow still here. That she was more than this picture and a body in the ground. Like maybe there was another part to her— a soul—and maybe that part was still out there. And if her soul was still there, then maybe, just like those nuns had spoken to the dead pope, Iris could find some way to communicate with Sarah.

So, Pigeon, how'd it go?" Iris's dad slid out from under the kitchen sink, where he was attempting to install a garbage disposal.

"I emptied half the boxes," Iris said. "That's all I'm going to do today." She spoke defensively, ready to fight if he said she had to finish.

But all he said was "Good progress." He slid back under the sink. "Hand me that smaller wrench, will you?"

Iris looked around. There, on the table, partially obscured by the newspaper, was the wrench. She handed it to her dad and then got some cookies before sliding into a chair at the table.

"How's it going?" she asked.

"Home ownership is a privilege and a joy," he answered, but Iris heard that tone in his voice that meant he was only half serious.

She munched through her first cookie before asking, "Dad?"

"Hmm?"

"Do you believe that a person has a soul?"

He laughed. "That's a big question for a Saturday morning, Pigeon."

"Well," said Iris, "do you?"

Her dad stopped thumping at the pipes. He was still for a moment before he slid back out. Sitting up, he scratched his head with the wrench. "You know," he began, "I didn't used to. Before you were born. But after I met you . . ." He shook his head and smiled. "I don't know, Pigeon. I never cared much about that sort of thing—I figured that when I died, that would be that, and honestly, that was all right with me. But since becoming a dad, I guess I've gotten softer. Because I can't imagine that *you* won't still be around after you die, you know, one day far in the future when you're a hundred and fifty or so. That I just can't bring myself to believe." His eyes looked misty for a minute, and his gaze drifted off to the side. Then he cleared his throat, spun the wrench in his hand.

Iris didn't like thinking about dying, even if it did happen when she was one hundred and fifty. It occurred to her that if she lived to see a century and a half, both of her parents would most likely be long gone. And she didn't like thinking about *that,* either.

She rearranged her cookies, building a pyramid first and then a circle. "It seems like there should be some way to *know,*" she said.

"You're not the first to wonder, that's for sure," said her dad. "Did you ever hear about Dr. Duncan MacDougall?"

Iris shook her head.

"Toss me one of those cookies," he said.

She did. He bit into it and continued: "He's probably a crackpot, but it's an interesting story. So back in the early 1900s, Dr. Duncan MacDougall tried to prove that there really is such a thing as a soul. He thought if he could show that a soul had mass—that it *weighed something*—then people would have to agree that it was a real thing. So he built this special bed in his office, and he got volunteers—dying people—and one by one, as they got close to their end, he laid them in the bed and waited for them to die, weighing them before and after. He figured if their weight dropped after death, that would be proof that their souls had left their bodies." He paused here, a worried expression wrinkling his brow. "Is this too morbid for you, Pigeon?"

Iris shook her head. "So? How much does it weigh?"

Her dad laughed. "You sound like you're already convinced that it weighs something."

Iris thought about Sarah. About how one moment she had been fine, perfectly fine, and the next moment, she had not. It was just too hard to believe that, because her body had ceased to work, there was no more Sarah at all in the world. It just couldn't be true. There had been too much to Sarah—too much life, too much wonderfulness, for all of her to go away, all at once.

"It must weigh something," she said firmly.

"The good doctor agreed with you," her dad said. "According to his calculations, the weight of the soul is three-quarters of an ounce."

"So there you go!" said Iris, triumphant. "Proof!"

"Slow down, Pigeon," cautioned her dad. "You know science is never that easy. He only had six subjects, and his results were only clear with a couple of them."

"But still," argued Iris, "it must mean *something*."

Her dad shrugged. "Maybe," he said. "Maybe not. Want to know what I think?"

Iris shrugged.

"*I* think," he said, "that people see what they're looking for. Especially when they're afraid of seeing anything else."

Iris felt her face scrunch up. She didn't answer.

"I *also* think," her dad continued, "that the garbage disposal is one of humankind's most clever inventions. And the homestead will be greatly improved if I can get this thing installed. What do you say? Want to be my assistant? See if you can make sense of these instructions?" He pointed the wrench at a crumpled-up manual on the floor.

"Okay," said Iris. But though she read the instructions and helped her dad install the disposal, her mind wasn't really there. A secret voice sang inside her heart: *The soul has weight.* She was thinking about Sarah, and souls, and the blossoming of hope she felt in her chest. If Sarah was out there, then Iris was going to find her.

9

We should be partners for the science project," Boris said. He and Iris were waiting for the bus; it was late. They crowded together with the rest of the kids who took the bus, just inside the back door of the gym, where they waited on the rainiest days. The sky was so fiercely dark with clouds that it felt like it should be bedtime.

Iris shrugged. "Why not."

"We could write about Linus Pauling," Boris suggested, "the guy our school is named after."

"Uh-huh," said Iris. She wasn't really listening. She was watching Starla and Isobel. They didn't look anything alike, they didn't even dress the same, but still, it was clear as could be that they were best friends. Starla pulled out a pack of gum. Iris could see there was just one piece left.

"Do you know anything about Linus Pauling?"

"Uh-uh," said Iris, her attention still on the girls. Without hesitation, Starla tore the piece of gum in two and handed half to Isobel.

The bus arrived at last. The driver smiled at them as they climbed aboard. "Sorry I'm late," she told them, once the bus was full. "There was a problem with the battery."

"That's all right, Mrs. Kassab," said Boris. "Thanks for the ride."

There were snickers, of course, from some of the other kids. Why was it, Iris wondered, that politeness was so funny to some people?

"Better watch out, Iris," came a voice. "Looks like your boyfriend has a thing for the Casaba Melon."

So much was embarrassing about this taunt, coming from the back of the bus. The boyfriend thing, of course, and the terrible nickname the older kids had started calling Mrs. Kassab since it had become obvious that she was pregnant, her belly pushing out round and hard against the flowered tops she wore over khaki slacks.

Iris knew that Mrs. Kassab didn't like the nickname, even though she always laughed when she heard the kids say it. Iris knew because of the way Mrs. Kassab's hands tightened on the steering wheel, the way she shoved the long gearshift into position rather than easing it into place as she usually did.

Next to her, Boris was busy punching words into his phone, browsing articles, it looked like.

"What are you doing?" Iris asked.

"Did you know that Linus Pauling is the only person who has ever won two unshared Nobel Prizes?"

"I told you, I don't even know who Linus Pauling *is,*" Iris said, irritated.

"*Was,* actually," said Boris, his eyes scanning the tiny lines of text on his phone's screen. "He died in 1994. He was ninety-three years old."

"Interesting," said Iris, but Boris missed the sarcasm in her tone.

"He was an interesting guy," he said. "It says here that when he was eleven years old—our age—he underwent a religious crisis. He decided that the miracle stories in the Bible couldn't be true, and he became an atheist."

Upon hearing the word "miracle," Iris found herself begrudgingly engaged. "What else does it say?" she asked.

"He was a chemist," read Boris, "and a peace activist. That was what he won his awards for—chemistry and peace activism. But I guess later on he got kind of wacky—he wrote all this stuff about vitamin C and how it could maybe cure cancer. Some people call him a quack."

"So, then, he could have been wrong," said Iris. "About other things."

"What other things?"

"About miracles not being real. Maybe he wasn't right about that, even if he was a scientist, if he was wrong about the vitamin C thing."

"Vitamin C is super good for you," Boris said.

"But not as good as a miracle," Iris answered.

"What's up with you and miracles?"

"I heard about this other scientist," Iris said, ignoring Boris's question. "My dad told me about him. He wanted to prove that people really do have souls, so he weighed people before and after they died to see if they got any lighter, to show their souls left their bodies."

"Creepy."

"If souls are real, though," said Iris, "then maybe miracles are real too. You know, like your miracle?"

Boris shrugged, pocketed his phone.

"You look like you don't care about it," said Iris. She felt angry.

"About what?"

"Miracles," said Iris. "Whether they're real."

"The way I figure," said Boris, pushing up his glasses, "it doesn't really matter."

Now Iris felt furious. "I don't know how *you* of all people can say that."

"What *I* don't get," said Boris, "is why it's such a big deal to *you*."

"Forget it," Iris said.

The bus screeched to a stop by Boris's neighborhood. The sound of the falling rain intensified as Mrs. Kassab pulled the lever to open the doors.

"Wanna come over?" Boris asked, standing.

"Nah," said Iris. "See you tomorrow."

Boris looked concerned. Iris could tell that he wanted to stay and figure out what was the matter, but then his shoulders drooped a little, and he said, "See ya," before heading out into the rain. Iris was still irritated, but watching Boris walk down the street as the bus pulled away, she wished she had been more kind.

At the second-to-last stop, after the only other kid had gotten off the bus, Iris scooted up to the seat behind Mrs. Kassab. Iris didn't really want to talk, but she felt kind of bad about the other kids calling the driver Casaba Melon, and it seemed like the nice thing to do.

"How much longer until your baby comes?" she asked.

Mrs. Kassab patted her belly. "Five more months," she said. "In the spring."

"That sounds like a good time to have a baby," Iris said, being polite.

"Absolutely perfect," said Mrs. Kassab. "I will take a leave from my work in the spring, and will have the summer to focus on my new son."

"Oh, it's a boy?" Iris asked.

Mrs. Kassab laughed. "Well, I *think* he is a boy. My husband doesn't want to find out. He says it's supposed to be a surprise. But I cheated a little."

"Did you get an ultrasound?"

"Well, yes, we had an ultrasound, and the baby is perfectly healthy, but we told the technician not to reveal the gender. So that's not how I cheated. But I did do something kind of crazy." She smiled. "Do you know what I did?"

Iris shook her head.

Mrs. Kassab met her gaze in the rearview mirror. "I visited a psychic." She sounded half embarrassed, half pleased. "She said the baby will be a boy." Then she held a finger to her lips. "Shhh," she said. "Don't tell anyone! My entire family would think I am nuts."

They had reached the homestead. Mrs. Kassab pushed the door lever, and Iris stood up. She didn't get off the bus, though, not right away. First, she asked, "Where did you find a psychic?"

"It wasn't hard," said Mrs. Kassab. "There is only one in town."

After dinner, while her parents played chess near the fire, Iris logged on to the computer to find the town's only psychic—Madame Occhiale. In her neatest writing, Iris printed the psychic's name, phone number, and address on the top sheet of the little yellow pad that her mother kept next to the computer. Then she carefully pulled the paper free from the rest of the pad, folded it in half, and slipped it into the pocket of her robe, all before her father called, "Pigeon! Your mother has beaten me again. Come tell her to take it easier on me."

As casually as she could, Iris went back to her parents, back to the warmth of the fire, her fingers curled around the folded-up paper in her pocket.

10

How long has it been since Sarah's death?"

Iris sat in between her parents on the orange couch in Dr. Shannon's office. It was a modern couch—low-backed, leather, with round metal legs. Dr. Shannon sat across from them in a blue velvet chair. Her suit was blue too—dark blue, with a knee-length skirt and a white button-down shirt underneath the jacket. Her hair was smoothed back into a low, neat bun.

She was too young to be any good at being a psychologist, Iris decided.

Behind Dr. Shannon was the room's one window. The sky, gray and clouded, rained and rained.

"It's been six months now," said Iris's father.

Dr. Shannon nodded and wrote in a little book.

"And you moved here . . ."

"Just over three months ago," said her mother. "I was hired by the infectious disease department at the university. Research."

This interested Dr. Shannon. Iris let herself tune out as her mom explained more about her job. Iris knew her mom did important work. She didn't need to hear it all again.

Actually, she hoped they'd keep talking about her mom's job for the whole hour. But instead, after just a few minutes, Dr. Shannon stood up. "You're welcome to wait in the lobby," she said as Iris's parents stood too. "Or there's a very good coffee shop down on the corner."

"Where are you going?"

"We're going to let you chat with Dr. Shannon for a while," her dad said. "We'll be back."

Iris considered putting up a fight. But she knew from her past experience with the psychiatrist in Seal Beach that it was a losing battle. So instead she just said, "Bring me a hot chocolate, okay?"

After Dr. Shannon had shut the door behind Iris's parents, she came back to the sitting area. But instead of returning to the blue chair, she sat on the other end of the couch, tucking one leg underneath herself and turning toward Iris.

Iris looked at her. Dr. Shannon smiled a little. "I'm so sorry about your friend," she said. "You must be terribly sad."

Iris opened her mouth to say something—she didn't know what—but instead of words, out flew a choked sob, and then her mouth crumpled, and she began to cry.

Dr. Shannon scooted closer and put a hand on Iris's back. She didn't rub or pat or try to stop Iris from crying, she just left her hand there. Iris cried long enough for the warmth of Dr. Shannon's hand to seep through her sweater and her T-shirt, all the way down to her skin. And it was such a relief, to cry like this, without worrying that her parents might hear her. She had never cried in the old psychiatrist's office; maybe it was because he always seemed to expect her tears, and Iris hadn't wanted to be that predictable.

But she cried now, and after a while she breathed in those ragged after-crying breaths that collapsed a few more times into tears, and then she wiped her eyes with her sleeve.

Dr. Shannon tilted a box of tissues toward her. Iris pulled out three, wiped her face again, blew her nose loudly.

"Sorry," she said.

"Absolutely nothing to apologize for," said Dr. Shannon. "Would you like some water?"

Iris nodded. Dr. Shannon left the room for a minute and came back with a bottle of water. She twisted off the cap before handing the bottle to Iris.

Iris gulped down half the water. "Thanks." She put the bottle on the low glass table next to the couch.

Dr. Shannon didn't ask any questions. She just waited, watching Iris calm herself down, but not in a creepy way. Iris decided that maybe Dr. Shannon wasn't completely terrible.

Finally, when Iris's breathing had calmed all the way down, when she'd blown her nose one last time, Dr. Shannon said, "Do you want to talk about it?"

Iris shook her head, but then she said, "I'm okay, you know? I mean, it isn't great or anything, but I'm okay. I'm taking care of Charles, and I made a friend, this kid named

Boris, and I'm not having any trouble sleeping anymore. Except just every now and then."

Dr. Shannon nodded. "Were you having trouble sleeping?"

"Yeah. I mean, at first. Right after. But now it's way better." Iris thought back to the first nights after they'd come home from the hospital, when Sarah hadn't.

She thought about how she'd spent each night wedged in between her parents, Charles on her chest, how she wouldn't dare to move in case it woke her parents up. She was afraid they might tell her to go back to her own bed.

"But you're sleeping better now."

"Yeah."

Neither of them said anything for a while. Then finally Iris decided to ask a question. "Dr. Shannon, do you believe in miracles?"

Dr. Shannon's face didn't reveal any surprise about the new direction the conversation was taking. "That depends," she said. "What exactly do you mean by miracles?"

Iris told her about Boris. About how he was supposed to die, but didn't.

"What a wonderful way for that to have turned out," Dr. Shannon said.

"But do you think it's a miracle?"

Dr. Shannon shrugged. "What do you think?"

Iris thought about it for a moment. "I looked up 'miracle,'" she said. "*Wikipedia* says a miracle is an event attributed to divine intervention. So something is only miraculous if it's because God made it happen."

"That's interesting."

"Yeah," said Iris. "But what I want to know is, if there *is* a God . . . if divine intervention is possible . . . then why would miracles only happen sometimes? Wouldn't it make more sense, if God could make good things happen, that miracles would happen all the time?"

"Like with Sarah," Dr. Shannon said. "I'll bet you wonder why there wasn't a miracle for her."

Dr. Shannon was smart, Iris decided.

"Well," Dr. Shannon went on, "what do you think? Why wasn't there a miracle for Sarah?"

Iris thought for a long time before she spoke again. She wasn't sure how much she wanted to tell Dr. Shannon. Mostly she was afraid—she didn't want this blue-suited psychologist to tell her that she was crazy, or that she was making things up, or that the thing that she wanted was impossible.

But finally Iris said, "I think maybe Sarah *did* get a miracle."

"Ah," said Dr. Shannon. She didn't sound surprised, and she didn't laugh, either.

Iris went on. "I think Sarah might be a ghost."

Dr. Shannon still didn't say anything. She just nodded.

Iris continued, encouraged. "I think she's a ghost, like a floating soul, and I think she came with us from California. I think she's in our house. Our new house. And I think she wants my help."

"What do you think she needs?"

"I don't know." Iris was talking faster now. "She hasn't said anything to me yet. But I *feel* her there. It's like she's right around the corner. Like she just stepped out of the room and she'll be right back. It's like she's listening."

Iris waited for Dr. Shannon to say something.

"Well?" Iris said at last. "What do you think?"

"I think," said Dr. Shannon, "that you really miss your friend."

Iris decided that maybe Dr. Shannon wasn't so wonderful after all.

When their appointment was over, Iris's parents took her to American Dream Pizza. It reminded her of when she was a little kid and they would take her to Chuck E. Cheese's after she'd get an immunization, to take the sting out of it.

The parking lot was completely packed; they'd had to leave the car around the corner and had run through the rain together, her father holding open the door while Iris and her mom ducked inside. The long wooden benches and booths were all crammed with people laughing and eating and talking loudly over each other and over the music that blared. All the noise made Iris's heart pound, and she wished her parents would just get the pizza to go. A girl took orders from the long line. The sleeves of her AMERICAN DREAM PIZZA T-shirt were pushed up, revealing colorful tattoos on both of her forearms. And Iris didn't think that her hair, black that shined blue when the light hit it, was a color that was found naturally on anyone.

They joined the line, inching slowly forward. When it was their turn, Iris's mom ordered. "We'll have a large Dream Special and a pitcher of root beer, please."

The girl rang them up. Iris couldn't take her eyes off

her tattoos. Her left arm had a tree with an enormous green canopy and stretchy brown roots; her right arm had a snake curved into a figure eight, its tail disappearing into its mouth.

The girl smiled at Iris. "Hey, little lady," she said. "I've never seen you in here before."

"We're new in town," said Iris's mother.

"Oh, yeah? How are you liking it so far?" The girl spoke to Iris, not her mom.

Iris shrugged. "It rains a lot."

The girl laughed loudly, like Iris had said something really funny. "That it does, my friend."

They took their pitcher and three cups and wedged themselves in at the end of one of the long benches. Everyone else at the table seemed to know each other; it looked like a birthday party: a bunch of balloons were tied to a table leg, and a plastic box of cupcakes was off to one side.

In fact, the whole place felt like a party.

Iris's dad struck up a conversation with the man sitting across from him. "Is it always so busy in here?" he asked.

"The pizza's great," said the man. He took an enthusiastic bite of his slice as if to prove his point. A long strand of cheese dangled from his beard.

The little girl sitting next to Iris pointed at it and laughed. "Gross!"

The man swung his head to make the cheese string loop up, and he caught it in his mouth. The kids at the table erupted in a mixed cacophony of disgust and amazement.

That girl Heather, who'd tried to sit next to Iris on the bus, was in one of the booths. A woman in a medical uniform and two other kids, both boys, one older than Heather, a teenager, and one younger, maybe seven, were with her. Iris wondered where their dad was, if maybe Heather's parents were divorced. Maybe Heather's dad had left them after the youngest kid was born because he'd wanted to start a rock band and Heather's mom didn't want him to. Maybe he'd decided that he'd rather have his music than his family. And maybe Heather called his phone all the time but he never answered. Maybe Heather had a big black hole right in the center of her where her dad had been.

Heather caught Iris staring at them and waved, but

Iris pretended to be looking at something on the wall behind her.

"Do you know that girl?" Iris's mom asked. "From school?"

Iris shrugged. "We have a couple of classes together."

"We should invite her to come sit with us," her dad said in that voice he used when he was having a *great idea* that wasn't great at all.

"I don't think so," Iris said. Her dad looked like he wanted to insist, but then he didn't.

Iris half listened as her dad told her mom about the pros and cons of solar panels and wind turbines. "Lots of local folks have solar panels," he said, "but I really think a turbine might be the way to go, at least to start. We could invest in a nine-hundred-watt unit. It would have a seven-foot turbine—probably not big enough to power all our energy needs, but it would be something. And in a year or two, we could consider adding a few solar panels to the roof of the homestead."

"That sounds great, Frank," said Iris's mom.

A few minutes later, the door swung open and a man came in. He was tall and lean and more handsome than most dad-aged men. Heather waved at him, and he went over and slid into the booth next to her, leaning over first to kiss her mom.

No divorce. No rock band. No black hole.

At last their pizza came. Her dad asked for some ranch dressing so he could dip his slice. Iris had to admit, it really *was* the best pizza she'd ever had—just enough sauce, kind of tangy, loads of cheese. And the crust had been rolled in cornmeal, giving the outside a crunchy texture, while the center was soft and steamy warm.

Iris ate three pieces and drank two glasses of root beer.

After a while Heather and her family left with the rest of their pizza in a to-go box, and a different group of people sat down in the booth they'd occupied.

The kids at Iris's table offered her one of their cupcakes, and when they sang "Happy Birthday" to the birthday boy—who was turning six, he announced seriously—Iris and her parents joined in.

It was nice. The restaurant was warm and dry and fragrant, and though the rain pounded down outside, it was as cozy as Thanksgiving dinner inside American Dream Pizza.

11

It was a Thursday afternoon when Iris finally found both the nerve and the opportunity to walk over to Greeley Avenue, counting her way up the block until at last she saw the number that matched the one she'd printed on yellow lined paper.

It looked like a regular house, but there, in the front window, perched a little sign: PSYCHIC MEDIUM. INQUIRE WITHIN.

Iris took in the overgrown tree in the yard, its waterlogged roots breaking through the rich brown earth, its wealth of waxy green leaves, the shadow it cast over the whole front of the house. The front stoop had two chairs on it, each seat puddled with rainwater. As Iris climbed the steps to the door, she looked up to see fingers of gray light filtering through cracks in the small, pitched roof that shaded the porch. A pair of green rubber boots, the same kind that her dad wore to work in the garden, leaned upside down against the porch railing. Iris looked at their soles, at the raised numbers that marked their size, and a cold moment of unease washed across her. Not only were they the same kind of boots as her dad's, they were the exact same size, too.

Iris forced herself to relax. There was no way her father could be inside this house. First of all, Iris couldn't imagine that either of her parents would ever seek the counsel of a psychic; psychologists were definitely more their speed. And even if her dad ever *did* visit a psychic, what were the chances that he'd be here today, the one afternoon that Iris had failed to board the bus, instead walking toward town, her slicker shining wet, the ends of her braids soaked and wormlike against her shoulders?

Then Iris saw the thin iridescent line of a spider web ascending from the left boot to the railing's topmost rung, and her shoulders loosened. These boots were definitely not her dad's.

But were they a sign, then, some message from the universe that she shouldn't be here, that her parents would find out? Iris immediately dismissed this idea, reminding herself that she didn't believe in signs, and then admonished herself—*If you don't believe in signs, what are you doing here?*

At last she raised her hand to rap on the door, but just as she did, it swung open.

"I was wondering when you'd get up the nerve to knock," said the woman behind it. "Come on in out of the rain."

And then, all at once, several thoughts occurred to Iris. One, she wasn't supposed to go into strangers' houses. Two, no one—not her parents, not Boris—knew where she was. And three, this woman looked nothing like a psychic.

Not that Iris had ever seen a psychic before, in person. She'd seen them in movies, and they usually wore colorful turbans and lots of rings and long, flowing skirts. This woman looked just like a normal woman, nothing mystical about her in any way. Her hair, which was brown woven with streaks of gray, was up in a messy bun. She had on sweatpants and fuzzy blue slippers. There was a pencil tucked behind her ear and, Iris noticed, another shoved into her bun.

"Umm . . ." said Iris.

The woman's face crinkled. "Honey, are you lost?"

"I don't think so." Iris looked at the address she'd written on the yellow sheet of paper, then back at the numbers hanging beside the door. "I'm looking for someone . . . but maybe I have the wrong house?"

"Ah," said the woman. "You're looking for Madame Occhiale."

Iris nodded.

"Well," said the woman, "you found her. But my friends just call me Claude, short for Claudia."

Claude reached out her hand, and Iris shook it.

"Do you want to come inside?" asked Claude.

Iris felt foolish. She'd expected to find the psychic in an office or something, not a regular house, and she knew her parents would be furious if she went inside.

"I just want to ask you a question," she said at last.

"All right," said Claude. She loosened the tie on her sweater and wrapped it tighter, redoing the bow at her waist.

"Do you think you could tell me about my friend Sarah?" The words came with the sharp sting of tears that almost always went along with saying Sarah's name. "She's . . . not alive, anymore." It was hard enough to say that; Iris couldn't bring herself to say "Sarah's dead."

Claude sighed and scratched her head. Her bun tilted slightly. "You sure you won't come inside?"

"I don't think so," said Iris.

"All right, then. Just wait a minute."

It was more than a minute, but Iris wasn't in any position to complain, and when Claude returned, she brought two towels—one for each of the chairs—a couple of blankets, and a tray with a pot of tea, a sugar bowl, and two cups. Together Iris and Claude nestled into the now-dry chairs. An occasional drip of rain landed on Iris's head, but with a cup of tea in her hands and one of the blankets spread across her lap, she felt warm enough.

"My bus driver told me about you," Iris said, both by way of explanation and to make conversation. "She's pregnant, and you told her she was going to have a boy?"

"Oh, yes, I remember her," Claude said. "She was excited about the baby."

"Well," said Iris, feeling shy, "I was wondering if you could help me talk to my friend Sarah. If that's possible?"

Claude sipped her tea. "Do your parents know you're here?"

Iris shook her head. "My parents don't believe in this stuff," she said apologetically.

"I see. But you do?"

Iris shrugged. "I don't know," she said. "Maybe?" She thought about the Catholic Church, how they believed in miracles. She thought about the weight of the soul. She thought about Linus Pauling, how he dismissed all of it and focused his life on science and the potential benefits of high vitamin C consumption.

"When I was your age," said Claude, "I didn't have many friends."

"Why not?"

Claude laughed. "Not many kids want to be friends with the girl who says she can talk to ghosts," she answered. "Plus, I had a really hard time trusting people."

"How come?"

"I think it's because when I was eight or so, I had this one friend named Nona. God, I loved her. She had curly hair, and glasses, and she was the first friend who seemed as excited to see me as I was to see her. You know?"

Iris thought about Sarah. About how their friendship had felt so equal, like two balanced sides of one scale. She nodded.

"But then I got sick," said Claude. She was holding her tea, and she was talking to Iris, but she was staring out into the rain as if she were seeing something far away and long lost. "I had to have my tonsils out, and I missed school for three weeks. And when I came back, Nona had made friends with this group of girls—the popular girls, I guess—and she wouldn't have anything to do with me. When I got upset and demanded an explanation, all she said was that I was weird." Claude was quiet for a minute, still staring off into space, and then her gaze snapped back to the present, to Iris.

"I'm sorry," Iris said.

"Me too," said Claude. "Nona and I had a lot of fun together, before that."

"Did you ever go back to being friends?"

Claude shook her head. "Nona's family moved the next summer. I never saw her again."

Iris wasn't sure what Claude's story had to do with her. "So," she said, "can you help me talk to Sarah? Is that something you can do?"

Claude looked at Iris for a minute. "It's something people pay me to do," she said at last.

A wave of embarrassment hit Iris hard. "Oh," she said. "Yeah, I know. I mean . . . how much do you charge?" Here she was, sitting and drinking tea and talking with this stranger like they were friends, like Claude *wanted* to talk with her, when all this time she had been waiting for Iris to pay her. It was like Dr. Shannon—she got paid, too, for talking with Iris, only Iris's parents took care of that bill.

"Usually I charge seventy-five dollars for a session that searches to connect with a lost loved one," Claude answered. "But that's not what I meant. That is, I don't want you to give me any money."

That was a relief, Iris thought, because she had nowhere *near* seventy-five dollars in her backpack.

"Let's just drink our tea," Claude suggested, "and we can chat a while."

That didn't sound like an ironclad promise to connect with Sarah, but since Iris didn't have enough money to pay Claude anyway, she just nodded and took another sip of tea. It was floral and sweet. Even in the middle of this rain and cold, it reminded her of springtime.

"Friends," Claude suddenly said, after an uncomfortable length of time had passed, "leave our lives in all different ways. My friend Nona's leave-taking was not ideal, and certainly your friend Sarah's wasn't either. But this is what I think: We don't get to choose how or when our friends leave us. We don't even get to choose *whether* they leave us. But we do get some say over the stories we remember."

"Uh-huh," said Iris, being polite. This wasn't much different from what everyone else told her—that she needed to remember the good times with Sarah, that she could keep Sarah alive with her thoughts. But then, almost without meaning to, she asked, "Weren't you angry?"

"Angry?"

"Yeah. When Nona ditched you. For the other kids. Didn't that make you mad?"

Claude blinked. She lifted her teacup, then set it down again in its saucer. "At first, I couldn't believe it had happened. That Nona had really left me like that. Then I was sad. Terribly, heartbrokenly sad. But later . . . yes. Later I was mad as hell."

Iris nodded. She felt mad too. Mad for this woman, Claude, who did seem kind of weird but couldn't have deserved to be dumped like that.

"Are *you* angry?" asked Claude.

"Me? Why would I be angry?"

"Well," said Claude, "your friend left you, too, didn't she?"

"It wasn't like that," said Iris, feeling her heart beating faster. "Sarah didn't *want* to leave."

"But still," said Claude.

Iris felt hot, suddenly, in spite of the wet air, and the blanket on her lap seemed to smother her. She was sorry she'd come, angry with herself for this whole encounter, and angry with Claude, too, even though she'd been pretty nice, considering how Iris had just shown up. "I've got to get home," Iris said, and her teacup clattered against its saucer as she set it down. The blanket fell to the porch's wet wooden slats as she stood, but she didn't pick it up. "It was stupid of me to come here," she said. "Sorry I bothered you."

And she fled the psychic's house, the rumble of thunder drowning out whatever Claude called to her, words that later Iris would think might have been, "I'm sorry."

That night, as Iris and her parents were doing the dishes after dinner, Boris called. "It's me," he said in a spy-whisper, even though Iris's dad had already announced, "It's Boris," as he handed her the phone.

"Hi," she answered. She folded and unfolded the red dishtowel, the phone tucked against her shoulder.

"Listen," Boris said, "I don't know where you were this afternoon, but your mother called my house looking for you, and I told her you were at the library doing research for our Linus Pauling paper."

"Okay," said Iris, trying to keep her tone neutral, in case her parents were listening. "Thanks."

"But tomorrow," he continued, "you have to tell me where you really were."

"See you on the bus," Iris answered, and she hung up.

So Iris wasn't surprised when the next morning Boris barreled down the aisle of the bus like an eager Labrador.

"Well?" He flopped down next to her, shoving his backpack on the floor between his rain boots.

Iris really didn't want to tell him about visiting Claude the psychic. She didn't want to think about it—about the visit, or the tea, about what Claude had said about being angry. But Boris had covered for her; she owed him something for that. So briefly, Iris recapped their conversation.

"Wow," said Boris. Then, "What kind of a name is Claude?"

"It doesn't matter," Iris said, annoyed that Boris managed to focus on the most insignificant detail of the whole thing.

After a minute Boris asked, "So do you think you can, like, talk with Sarah? I mean, for real?"

"It's not all that different from what the Vatican thinks about you," she said. "About how those nuns talked to that dead pope."

Boris shrugged. Iris knew he hated talking about all that.

"Maybe," he said. They didn't say anything for a few minutes. The bus was quieter than usual. The days were growing shorter, and mornings were darker.

Then, like a bone he couldn't drop, Boris brought it up again. "It could be pretty neat," he said. "Trying to contact someone who isn't alive. I mean, Linus Pauling probably wouldn't approve, but still . . . it's sort of like a science experiment. Can I help?"

Iris's first instinct was to say no. But instead she asked cautiously, "You'd take it seriously? You won't make fun of me?"

"Uh-uh!" Boris sounded insulted.

"Okay, then," she said, and immediately regretted it when Boris started bouncing in his seat. But maybe it wouldn't hurt to have someone helping her out. After all, the thing with the psychic had been kind of a flop.

"This reminds me of Magic," Boris said conspiratorially as they disembarked in front of the school a few minutes later.

"Everything reminds you of Magic."

"It's like when one of your best cards gets stuck in your graveyard, and you can't play it anymore, and then you draw an Adun Oakenshield."

"What's an Adun Oakenshield?" Iris was curious, in spite of herself.

"It's a Legendary Creature. A Human Knight. If you

draw it, you can return one card from your graveyard to your hand, back into play. There are a bunch of cards that let you do that. I have one at home. I'll show it to you next time you come over. Wanna come over today? After school?"

"Sure," said Iris, feeling generous. And maybe it would be all right to have Boris helping her. After all, if Boris really was a miracle, then it couldn't hurt to have him on her side.

12

"We've got to make a plan," Boris said that afternoon, pacing in the kitchen while Iris perused the snack possibilities at his house. Pre-sliced red peppers and baby carrots, she decided, with ranch dressing. Later, maybe she'd come back for snack dessert.

"Uh-huh," she said. "A plan is good."

Boris watched as Iris assembled her snack platter. "Throw some crackers on there too. And some cheese slices," he said. "We can share."

Ugh. Sharing a snack with Boris. Iris felt her appetite waning, but she added the cheese and crackers, pushing them to the far edge of the plate.

"Come on," Boris said. "We'll see what we can find on the computer."

Iris followed Boris down the hall to his bedroom. He dumped his backpack on the bed and pushed his laptop to one side of the desk to make room for the snacks. "Get another chair from the twins' room," he ordered, and flopped himself into his chair in front of the computer. He opened the laptop and began tapping the space bar impatiently, waiting for the computer to start up.

Iris almost said something about manners, but then decided it would be a waste of energy. Instead she slid the tray of food next to the computer. Boris dug right in, dunking a carrot into the dressing and slicing it in half with his teeth, chewing loudly. He was, Iris noticed with a tiny shudder, a double dipper. Iris went in search of a chair.

The twins weren't home, and Iris found a chair on the clean side of their room. There may have been a matching chair on the other side, but it was difficult to be certain, draped as it was by sweaters and jeans and something that looked alarmingly like a banana peel.

"There are over one billion results when you Google

'talking to the dead,'" Boris told Iris when she reentered his room with a chair. She dumped it with a clatter next to Boris, but he didn't get the hint. He didn't even look up.

Iris sat. A billion results. The number terrified her. "We'll never sort through all those," she said. "It would take a lifetime."

Boris looked over at her, chewing. "You say that like it's a bad thing."

"It *is* a bad thing."

He shook his head. He looked, Iris thought, like a spaniel shaking water off its coat. "No way," he said. "It's a *great* thing. Over a billion results . . . One of them's got to be something good."

It could be, Iris considered, that Boris actually had a point. One billion results . . . If each result was a lottery ticket, then one of them was bound to be a winner. "Okay," she said, grabbing a red-pepper slice. "Let's see what we can find."

A n hour later, all that was left of the snack platter were crumbs and one sad baby carrot, half drowned in the remaining ranch dressing. Iris had kicked off her shoes, and she sat cross-legged next to Boris, her science notebook open on her lap. They had made a list.

Out of the billion results that their Google search had yielded, Iris figured that they had skimmed through at least a thousand. Maybe more. Most of them, of course, were ridiculous. Some of them were pretty scary.

Boris had gotten especially creeped out when he read some of the stuff the Bible had to say about contacting the dead. "Look at this," he'd said, after clicking on a link to Leviticus, a book of the Bible. He turned the computer toward Iris.

"Men and women among you who act as mediums or psychics must be put to death by stoning. They are guilty of a capital offense," she read out loud. "That doesn't sound great. Does it worry you? I mean, if you don't want to help me . . ."

"No, no, I'm totally going to help you," Boris said. "It's just sort of weird, you know? Because the nuns who prayed to that dead pope to save me . . . Wasn't that like talking to the dead? And *that* was okay. With the church, I mean."

Iris shrugged. She hadn't even known what a pope

was, all that long ago. She wasn't the right person for questions about that. But still, what if it *was* dangerous to try to talk to Sarah? Not stoning-dangerous, but maybe some other kind of dangerous. Something she couldn't imagine.

"Maybe this is a bad idea," she said.

"Uh-uh," said Boris. "If a bunch of old nuns feel safe talking to the dead, then how bad of an idea could it be?"

Every now and then, Iris thought, Boris said something really, really smart.

"This one looked pretty cool." Iris tapped her pencil against the first thing she'd written. "EVP."

"Which one is that, again?"

"It's short for electronic voice phenomena. It's the idea that the dead are still here, right around us, and it's only because our ears aren't sensitive enough that we can't hear them talk."

"Oh, yeah," said Boris. "That one did sound neat. We could try it right now, if you want."

Iris shook her head. "We need to learn more about it first," she said. She considered telling Boris about Sarah's ghost, how sometimes it felt like she was there, at the homestead, under the stairs. But that felt like too fragile a secret to share. "And when we try it, we should do it at my place."

"Okay," said Boris. "I'll research it."

Iris wrote his name next to *EVP*. And underneath that, next to *Mirror Gazing,* she wrote her own name. Then she said, "Maybe we could try to find out more about the Catholics, too. Since you got that miracle, and all. Maybe we could learn about how those nuns contacted the dead pope."

"I think they just *prayed* to him," Boris said.

"I know," said Iris. "But I mean, why did *that* prayer work? Lots of people pray for stuff, and they don't get miracles."

"I guess I could ask the Vatican guys, when they come to visit," said Boris, but he sounded dubious.

Iris wondered about the people from the Vatican, what they would look like, what kind of answers they might have. "Yeah, maybe," said Iris. But she thought, *Maybe I can ask them myself.*

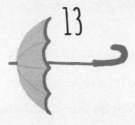

13

The list grew. Some of the ideas were silly—*Ouija Board, Crystal Ball*—and Iris dismissed them almost as soon as they were written down. Others were scary—*Visit a Graveyard, Hold a Séance*—and Iris considered these to be last-resort ideas. Boris was enthusiastic about what he had started to call "The Ghost Project" in a way that Iris found increasingly irritating, especially once winter break began and they had whole days together.

"I don't think we should give up on the idea of a séance quite yet," Boris told Iris on the second day of vacation. The two of them were wandering around downtown, poking into various shops. Boris needed to buy Christmas presents for all of his sisters, and Iris wanted to get something for her parents. Each store they went into had a bucket by the entrance for umbrellas, and a rack for hats and jackets. Most of them also had a large rubber mat just inside the door.

"A séance just sounds creepy." Iris picked up a ceramic cabbage and turned it over, enjoying its cool smoothness against her palm. Maybe she could start a collection of glass vegetables for her dad. Then she saw the price, $17.95, and she put it back down.

"The whole thing is creepy, though, isn't it?" He sounded eager. Too eager, Iris thought.

"You don't get it," she said. "Sarah is my friend. This isn't some fun game, Boris, like Magic."

Next to her, Iris felt Boris deflate a little. He cleared his throat and adjusted his beanie. It was black and white striped, with a fuzzy ball on top. Iris stepped away and pretended to be really interested in a collection of shell figurines on the next shelf, but it was hard to see them through the tears that clouded her eyes.

A minute later, Boris walked up behind her. She felt his hot breath on her ear.

"Hey, Iris," he said. "I'm really sorry."

She lifted and dropped her shoulders in answer.

"I guess I just get excited about things," Boris said. "And I want to help."

"It's okay," Iris said. "But Sarah isn't creepy."

"I know," Boris said. "She was your best friend."

Iris nodded.

"What was she like?"

Iris considered this question. She wanted to remember everything about Sarah, wanted to hold on tightly to all of her—the way she could raise one eyebrow and then the other, the sound of her laugh, the joy she found in winning—but so much of Sarah was already gone. And Iris worried that if she shared anything about Sarah with Boris, she would halve what little she had left.

Later, sitting with Dr. Shannon, Iris shared this concern. She left out the stuff about trying to communicate with Sarah; Dr. Shannon didn't need to know *everything*. But she did tell Dr. Shannon that she felt like she was sort of cheating on Sarah. By hanging out with Boris. By having another friend.

Dr. Shannon nodded, but didn't answer at first. She passed Iris the ever-present box of tissues, and she waited for Iris to blow her nose. Then she said, "When

I was about your age, my parents got a divorce. My dad didn't remarry, not right away, but my mom did. She married a man named Paul, who became my stepfather. I was pretty angry about the divorce, but even more I was upset on my father's behalf that he had been replaced so quickly. That's what it felt like—that he'd been replaced."

Iris took another tissue and shredded it in her lap.

"I didn't want to like Paul. And I didn't want Paul to like me. I was actually pretty rude to him." Dr. Shannon smiled, remembering. "I used to hide his shoes," she confessed. "Not whole pairs, just the left ones. There was a panel in the ceiling of my bedroom closet that accessed the attic, and I would push that aside and throw Paul's left shoes up there. Not all the time—that would have been too obvious. Just every now and then. I don't know if they suspected me right away, or if it took them a while to figure out that I was the culprit, but Paul never yelled at me or even confronted me about it. He just kept buying more shoes."

"Did you ever give them back?" Iris asked. "The shoes?"

"I did," Dr. Shannon said.

"When?"

"When my father got engaged to his next-door neigh-bor," Dr. Shannon said. "About eighteen months later."

"Did he say anything then? Paul, I mean?"

"Nope," said Dr. Shannon. "Not even then. He never said a word about the shoes."

Iris thought about the stories grownups had been tell-ing her lately about leave-takings. She thought of Claude, about how her best friend had abandoned her. She con-sidered Dr. Shannon's parents, and how their separation must have felt to Dr. Shannon.

There were, Iris felt, so many ways for a heart to break.

When Iris got home, she called Boris. When he came to the phone, without even saying hello, she told him, "Sarah was funny, and smart, too. And she was brave." Iris could hear Boris breathing on the other end of the line. Then she said, "Back home, our teacher, Mrs. Pres-ton, used to post all our test grades up at the front of the class, right next to our names, from best to worst."

"Huh," said Boris.

"She thought it was a good way to encourage us to do better. And this one time, after our U.S. geography test— we had to fill in the names of all the states and capitals on a blank map—this kid, Jimmy Dermer, his name was right at the bottom, dead last."

"I guess someone had to be," said Boris.

Iris ignored the interruption. "He was doing that thing when you have to cry but you don't want anyone to notice—where you pretend that you're rubbing your eyes because you're tired but really it's to keep the tears from falling. No one was paying any attention to him, anyway. They were all too worried about their own place on the list to care about Jimmy. And you know my friend Sarah?"

Boris was silent, but Iris could feel that his silence had weight. "Sarah's name was the first one," she went on. "She got one hundred percent, plus extra credit for writing in the names of all the state birds. That's how she was . . . super competitive, and smart. Anyway, she didn't notice Jimmy either, but I pointed him out to her."

"Then what happened?" Boris asked.

"She went right up to Mrs. Preston and told her to take down the list. Sarah said that if Mrs. Preston didn't take it down, she would start a petition to make her, because it was illegal in the state of California to post students' private information, like grades and stuff, without their permission."

"Was that true?"

"Who knows?" Iris said. "But since Sarah had just scored a hundred and ten percent on a test all about the states, I guess Mrs. Preston believed her. She went over and untacked the whole list, and that was the last time she ever posted our grades."

"That was pretty cool of Sarah, considering her name was at the top of the list," Boris said.

"That's just the way she was," Iris said. "Sarah took care of business."

After a minute, Boris said, "Hey, Iris?"

"What?"

"Thanks for calling."

14

⌈ all collapsed into winter. The days grew even colder
⌊ and darker. By early January, Iris's mom decided she
didn't want Iris riding the bus to school anymore.

"Black ice," she explained. "Too dangerous without
seat belts." So she or Iris's dad did the morning drive.

This at least let Iris sleep in an extra fifteen minutes,
which Charles appreciated. When she finally did have to
climb out of bed, she folded the blankets around him, up
over his ears to keep him warm.

On the first of February, Iris awoke to a different qual-
ity of light filtering through her bedroom window. She
slid out from underneath Charles's warm body, tucked
him in, and went to look outside.

All around was soft and white. Their car, parked next to the house, wore a coat of snow; the branches on the trees were bowed slightly with the weight of it.

Iris blinked against all the whiteness, it was so bright. And the *sky*—blue, painted with big, fluffy gray-white clouds. Iris hadn't seen a sky that blue since they'd arrived in Oregon.

Iris dressed quickly, pulling on her heaviest socks and her favorite jeans along with a thermal shirt and her thick purple wool sweater. And she bounded down the stairs two at a time, throwing open the front door and skidding to a stop on the porch.

She took a deep breath. The air filled her, cold and sharp. She bounced up and down, excited.

"Beautiful day," said her dad behind her. Iris turned and smiled at him.

He was wearing a sweater too. A funny zigzag-striped rainbow one. Steam from his coffee rose up, meeting the plumes of his breath. Her dad had started growing a beard when they moved to Oregon. It had been a funny beard at first, spotty in parts, but it was filling in pretty nicely, and Iris liked the way her father looked, standing there with his sweater and his coffee and his beard. He'd gotten a little thicker through the middle, too, from all the home-cooked meals he'd been preparing. Iris thought it suited him.

"Too pretty a day for school, I think," said her dad in a neutral tone of voice.

"Really?"

Her dad nodded. "Absolutely. First snow is a cause to celebrate. Come on inside. Let's eat some breakfast, and then I've got a surprise for you."

Her dad's waffles were always delicious, but Iris had a hard time concentrating on them this morning. She ate a few bites as she watched him bustle around the kitchen, packing a picnic lunch—a large thermos of hot chocolate, a smaller one of soup, a box of crackers, a plastic container of cheese and salami. Three plates.

"Is Mom coming with us?" Iris asked.

Her dad shook his head. "No, she had to go in to work early."

"So who's the third plate for?"

He smiled. "Not Charles."

They loaded the picnic into the old station wagon her

dad had bought for hauling gardening supplies. There was something in the far back, something long and lumpy, covered by a blanket.

"What's that?" Iris tried to peel back the blanket, but her dad grabbed the hood of her jacket and pulled her away.

"Wait and see," he sang. "Hop in."

They drove toward town, their tires crunching through snow. Iris's dad had wrapped them in chains and they clanked loudly.

"Where are we going?" Iris asked from the back seat.

"You'll see." Her father caught her gaze in the rear-view mirror. Iris loved the network of lines that crinkled around his eyes when he smiled.

Iris thought maybe they were going to the movies. Or to the bookstore. So she was surprised when they made the familiar turn into Boris's housing tract.

And there he was, waiting for them in his driveway— bundled up in a bright green jacket, a pair of thick black snow pants, boots. He wore his beanie, too.

Iris's dad honked two short, cheery blasts, and Boris waved. He ran to the curb as they pulled up, slipping once but regaining his footing before he hit the ground.

Iris slid across the back seat and opened the door for him.

"Hi, Iris. Hi, Frank," he said, grinning widely. "This is so much cooler than school. Thanks for inviting me!"

"It wouldn't be a party without Boris," her dad said. They pulled away from the house and turned onto the main street, heading back out of town.

"So where are we going?" Iris asked, feeling as if she might burst from the not-knowing.

Her dad pointed out the front window. "Yonder," he said. "Mary's Peak."

The sky stayed mostly clear as their car wound up Mary's Peak to its summit. Occasionally a thick gray cloud would drift in front of the sun; when it did, the world darkened into shadow until the cloud shifted again. Then sunlight sparkled on snow, reflecting starbursts like diamond light.

It took forty minutes before they finally pulled into the parking lot. A few other vehicles sat quiet in the snow, but there were no people in sight. Iris's dad twisted the key counterclockwise and the car ticked a little before it fell silent.

"Everybody out," he said.

Boris threw open his door and ran a few steps to an embankment of snow. He spread his arms wide, falling backwards, waving his arms and legs. "Snow angel!" he cried as he stood up.

Iris went around to the back of the station wagon and watched as her dad removed the blanket from the mystery lump she'd been wondering about the whole trip.

It was a sled—the cool old-fashioned kind, made of wooden slats screwed onto red metal runners. A length of rope formed a triangle at the front end, for steering. It was, Iris thought, a wonderful surprise.

"Awesome sled, Frank!" Boris fished a pair of mittens from his jacket pocket.

Iris's dad smiled at her. "So, what do you say? Ready?"

Iris pulled the sled by the rope handle to the end of the parking area. She made her way carefully around Boris's snow angel, making sure not to pass the runners across its shape.

Boris sledded every year with his sisters, he told them as they walked in search of a good slope, so he knew just what to look for. Not too steep, because that made climbing back up too much of a chore, and someplace wide with no trees in the way.

Iris was pretty sure she would have figured all that out on her own, but she didn't say anything to Boris. He seemed—as usual—to be enjoying his expertise.

She got more irritated, though, when Boris insisted that they pass up the first two spots that appeared to meet all his requirements. Finally Boris pointed to a slope not too far ahead. "There it is," he said, in a reverent tone. "The perfect slope."

They climbed the hill together, Iris's dad dragging the sled. Iris's boots crunched through the topmost snow, sending a shiver up her spine like when she pulled apart a cotton ball or when the teacher's chalk screeched across the board.

When they reached the top, all three of them stood for a minute breathing heavily. Iris was warm now, from the exertion of the climb, but she didn't want to take off her coat because she thought she might want it for the downhill sled ride. It took Iris's dad the longest to stop breathing so hard. When he finally did, he muttered, "Gotta get in better shape." He adjusted the sled so its nose pointed straight downhill. "Who's first?"

"I've done this lots of times," said Boris. "Let Iris go first."

Iris's dad gestured for her to climb on.

Suddenly the slope they'd climbed looked awfully steep. "I don't know about this," she said.

"Go on, Iris. It's fun," Boris said.

Iris stepped over to the sled and straddled it, sat down. Her dad handed her the steering rope. She looked up at him.

He must have seen the fear in her eyes, because he knelt down next to her. "You okay?"

"I don't know about this," Iris said again.

Her father nodded and stared down the hill. "It's pretty steep," he admitted.

"This is nothing!" Boris said. "You should *see* some of the hills I've sledded down. They're like cliffs compared to this!"

Iris's dad shook his head, and Boris shut up. Her dad

turned back to Iris. "Pigeon," he said, "no one's going to make you do this. We can walk the sled halfway down if you want, and you can try from there. Or you can watch Boris try it first."

Iris stared ahead at the snowy slope. Her tears fractured the light, making the snow gleam even more brightly. But when she answered him, her voice sounded strong to her own ears. "No," she said. "I've got this."

Her father grinned and patted her back. "That's my girl," he said, and stood. "Now, remember to keep the nose pointed downhill. Other than that, all you've got to do is hang on and have fun."

Iris nodded and wrapped the rope around her mitten-clad hands. She braced her feet against the front rail and made sure her weight was even. Then she said, "I'm ready."

That was enough for her dad, who gave her a push almost as soon as the words were out. At first the sled slipped slowly, and the back listed a little to one side, but after a couple of seconds it picked up speed, and then Iris was flying.

"Ohnoohnoohno!" she yelled, louder and louder as

the sled kept gaining speed, and then a lump of fear swallowed up her voice as the sled went even faster.

The white-powdered trees on either side of the slope whizzed by, blurring white-green-white in her peripheral vision. Her face felt icicle-cold, her fingers frozen into claws on the rope. There was the sound of the runners on the snow, of her father and Boris cheering above her, of her own ragged breaths. There was the shock to her spine of the sled's occasional bounce, the tightly wound muscles of her shoulders and neck, the frigid air as she gulped a breath.

And then, just before she reached the bottom, where the slope meandered into flatness, when everything else was still brilliantly, blindingly fast, and so purely *free* — nothing but speed and snow — a wave of pure joy washed through her and she smiled so widely that her cheeks grew sore.

Then the sled slowed, and slowed, and finally stopped. Iris blinked, swallowed, and turned to look back up the hill. Her dad and Boris were jumping, waving their arms wildly, and cheering.

Iris waved back triumphantly. She stood up on

shaking legs and waved again, turned her face toward the cold winter sky, and laughed out loud.

Later, after they'd eaten the picnic and drained the thermos of hot chocolate, when they'd each slid down the hill a dozen times or more, Iris, her dad, and Boris trudged back to the car. The clouds had thickened above them. Iris had worked up a sweat climbing the hill so many times, and as the air cooled, she began to shiver. Her father looped his arm over her shoulders. Boris trailed behind, dragging the sled. He was whistling, not a song or anything, just random notes strung together.

The clouds seemed to be deciding what to do next. Iris hoped that, just for a change, they'd decide to break apart and leave her in peace. She even thought the words *Please don't let it rain.* But of course it did.

When the first raindrop hit her face, Iris pretended not to notice. But then came a second, and then a rumble of thunder drowned out Boris's whistling, and the rain poured down.

"Run!" Boris yelled. He sounded panicked, like they were being chased by zombies, and Iris and her dad laughed and stumbled and ran the rest of the way to the car.

Iris's dad yanked open the hatch at the back of the station wagon. Boris and Iris hefted in the sled. Then they ran around to the side doors and slid into the back seat. Iris's dad slammed into the front, behind the wheel. The three of them sat and dripped and listened to the rain pound against the roof. It was so, so loud, and only then did Iris realize how peaceful the day had been, how quiet, without the constant thrumming of the rain.

As they pulled out of the lot, Iris's gaze landed on Boris's snow angel. The rain puddled in its center, and Iris saw their own footprints punched into its wings, crushing the side of its head.

15

"They've been married for twenty years," Boris told Iris. It was Friday, and Iris's dad had picked them both up from school to drive them to the homestead. "That's a long time. Neither set of my parents' parents was married that long, even though they were more Catholic than we are."

"Huh." Iris was only half listening. Most of her attention was focused on Boris's bright blue duffle bag, wedged between them in the back seat of the station wagon. Because of Boris's parents' twenty-year anniversary, his sisters were all spending the night with friends from school, and Boris would be staying at the homestead. He'd be the first guest to sleep in the spare bedroom, which reminded Iris of Sarah's favorite book, *Anne of Green Gables,* in which Anne had yearned to sleep in the "sparest of spare rooms."

This visit, they'd decided, would be the perfect chance to try EVP, and Iris knew that somewhere in that duffle bag was a digital voice recorder. "My dad bought it a year ago because he wanted to write a science-fiction novel," Boris had told Iris. "It was going to be about a race of aliens that came to Earth searching for the perfect companion animal. They were going to take a group of humans back to their planet, as pets, only then they find out that the humans have pets of their own, and that throws everything off. Like, can a pet have a pet? And if they take the humans to be their pets, should they bring the humans' pets along too? Anyway, he never really got started, and the recorder has just sat in the top drawer of his desk for the last nine months."

Iris had still never met Boris's father, but it seemed right to her that he should have science-fiction-novel-writing ambitions.

"I can't wait to see your place," Boris said to Iris's dad enthusiastically. "Iris never talks about it."

"What's there to say?" Iris asked. "It's a house. We live there."

Iris's dad laughed. "It's more than a house," he said. "It's the homestead. Boris, my boy, are you interested in home improvement? Restoration? Biosustainability?"

"I'm interested," Boris answered, "in everything."

And then the two of them launched into a lively conversation about manure, a topic Iris had no idea Boris knew anything about.

Iris ignored them and stared at her window, not through it, watching raindrops race down the pane of glass, watching as the wind swept them away. Some of the drops scattered easily, right after they'd fallen, but some of them left the windowpane not all at once, but rather little by little, tinier droplets breaking away until, inevitably, the pressure of the car's speed and the wind against them won, and the drops disappeared.

Her father turned the station wagon up the gravel driveway, and the tires made the crunching sound that Iris had come to identify with being almost home.

"There she is," her dad announced, turning off the car.

Iris appraised the farmhouse as she imagined Boris was doing beside her: its yellow wooden siding, in need of a fresh coat of paint ("In the spring," her dad had promised them); its perpetually rain-darkened shingle roof; the porch that wrapped around the house, strewn with gardening supplies; the tall white stacks of bagged fertilizer; the bikes no one had ridden since they'd been unloaded from the moving truck. And on the far edge of the property, the new wind turbine her dad had just had installed, his current pride and joy.

"Awesome," Boris said. "It looks like an old haunted mansion." He slid out of the car, forgetting his duffle bag, and completely oblivious, Iris thought, to what he had just said.

She collected her backpack and Boris's overnight bag, and followed him into the house.

Boris loved everything about the place: the steep staircase, the old woven rugs that Iris's dad had found at a nearby antique shop, the original O'Keefe & Merritt oven, the fireplace. And then he spied Charles, tucked into a corner of the couch, just his head visible from the woolly blanket that engulfed him.

"Whoa," said Boris. "Is that your cat?"

"This is Charles." Iris sat down gently beside him and scratched between his ears.

"He's even weirder-looking than I thought he'd be," Boris said. He didn't reach over to pet him.

"Charles thinks the same thing about you," Iris retorted, and Boris laughed.

All through dinner and dessert, Iris tried to act normal. Luckily, Boris was a fountain of conversation, and Iris didn't have to do much to blend in. As she listened to Boris telling her parents an animated story about how hard it was to be the only son in a family of girls, she thought about everything Boris had earnestly reported to her about his research into EVP.

"In 1952, two Catholic priests were recording Gregorian chants on this old machine called a Magnetophone," he'd said during lunch. "The wire kept breaking, and one of the priests looked up to heaven and asked his dead father to help. Later on when they listened to the recording, they heard the priest's father's voice say, 'Of course I shall help you. I am always with you.'"

It seemed to Iris that the Catholic Church kept itself pretty busy.

After dinner, Iris's mom suggested that they all watch a movie together, but Iris said, "No, thanks, we're going to play a game of Magic before we go to bed." She pulled her cards out of her backpack and made a good show of clearing off the kitchen table and shuffling the deck.

But after her mom said, "All right, you two. Have fun," and pushed through the kitchen's swinging door, Iris dropped her cards onto the table.

"Should I get the recorder?" Boris asked in a terribly loud whisper.

Iris nodded. "I found this cool article online," Boris had told her that morning on the bus. "It turns out that Thomas Edison, way back in the 1920s, was into electronic voice phenomena. He even tried to invent a machine that could pick up the voices of the dead. He never managed to do it, but he was pretty much a genius about electricity and stuff."

Iris listened to Boris's thumping footsteps as he ran up the stairs to the spare bedroom, then again as he ran back down. Slightly out of breath, Boris set the recorder on the table. He couldn't help but share its stats: "It's an Olympus. It has a four-gigabyte flash memory, up to one thousand and seven hours of recording time, and a USB 2.0 port. Usually it costs $199.99, but my dad got it on sale for thirty percent off."

Iris heard him, but only sort of. She felt a nervous flutter in her veins, and swallowed twice.

"Do you know what you're going to ask?"

Iris had written a list of questions, but she didn't need to retrieve it. Every question she had for Sarah was seared into her brain.

"Remember," Boris prompted, "after you ask the question, leave time for an answer. Just like you're having a conversation. And don't touch the recorder. Leave it flat on the table so you don't shake it around and accidentally cause sounds. And then after you're done, leave the recorder running. People on the Internet say that sometimes the ghosts, or whatever, say something more at the end."

Iris nodded again. Suddenly she wished Boris wasn't there, but he was. And this was the time—she could feel it. She reached out a shaky hand and pressed RECORD. A moment passed, and then Iris asked, "Sarah? Are you there?"

She waited a long moment, longer than it would take

anyone to say yes or no, and then she asked the next question. "Sarah? Are you okay?"

And that was when the tears began, and didn't stop, as she worked her way through the rest of the questions — *Did it hurt to die? Are you scared? Are you alone? Do you miss me? I miss you. Can you hear me?* Boris stood beside her awkwardly, and he patted her shoulder in his best attempt at comfort as she spoke, and waited, and spoke again, as her tears and dripping snot mingled together, as one blotchy tear smeared across a Magic card, a Reya Dawnbringer that Boris had given her, a Legendary Creature-Angel. The picture was filled with yellow light, and the broad-winged golden angel held a sword in her right hand. Beneath the picture were the words, "At the beginning of your upkeep, you may return target creature card from your graveyard to play." And beneath that, in italics, *"You have not died until I consent."*

Then Iris's questions were all asked, but still she didn't hit the button to end the recording. Together she and Boris waited in the kitchen, watching the digital clock on the Olympus show the seconds, the fractions of seconds, all the moments that they were there, and Sarah might be as well.

16

Iris stood in front of the door to the closet under the stairs. She counted again the six wood panels.

Down the hall in the kitchen, her parents were fooling around with the dishwasher. It had finally been installed that afternoon. Iris's mom was loading coffee mugs into the top rack, and her dad was reloading them into the other side, where he apparently thought they should go.

She heard her mother's warm, full laugh, and the cadence of her father's reply. Her parents, she realized, were another pair—like Starla and Isobel, like Boris's twin sisters. Like Iris and Sarah had been.

Iris held a book in her hands. It was tied around with one of her hair ribbons, red and white grosgrain.

The book's spine was maroon, embossed with gold. The cover read *Anne of Green Gables* in tall purple letters, and there was a picture of two girls—one dark-haired, the other with red braids—sitting under a tree, looking off into the distance.

It was an old copy of the book. Not first edition or anything, but not new, either. Iris had found it at Used and Valuable Books on Fourth Street. It had cost her thirty-three dollars exactly.

She had thirty dollars left over from Christmas, and Boris lent her the extra three. He didn't ask her what she needed the money for, or why she didn't get it from her parents. He just pulled the crinkled bills from his pocket and handed them over.

Since that night when they'd tried to record Sarah's voice, Boris had been even nicer to Iris than usual. Probably because when they'd listened to the recording the next morning, they had heard nothing in the pauses between Iris's questions. Or, not quite nothing, but certainly not Sarah's voice, not answers. The blank emptiness they did hear was, Iris felt certain, exactly what space would sound like if like one of the humans in

Boris's dad's unwritten science-fiction novel, she'd been collected by aliens to be their pet and been shuttled out of Earth's atmosphere, and into the wide boundlessness of the cosmos. A deep silence, darker and wider than Iris could completely fathom, in which there was nothing for sound waves to bounce off of, no way for them to return, only reams and reams of static nothing.

Today was Sarah's birthday. Or it would have been Sarah's birthday, if she had lived to see it. Iris wondered which verb tense was correct—was or would have been. Did you keep having birthdays after you were dead?

Sarah would be twelve. *Anne of Green Gables* had been her favorite book. She'd wanted Iris to love it as much as she did. And Iris liked it all right, but not as much as funnier stuff, or books with spies.

But when Iris had bought this book and secreted it home, she spent an hour flipping through its pages.

One part in particular reminded her of Sarah: "'Oh, it's delightful to have ambitions. I'm so glad I have such a lot. And there never seems to be any end to them—that's the best of it. Just as soon as you attain to one ambition you see another one glittering higher up still. It does make life so interesting.'"

Before she opened the closet, Iris peeked around the corner into the kitchen—her parents were still fiddling with the dishwasher.

Then Iris turned the door handle and peeked inside.

The closet was musty and dark. There were the coats on the hangers. There was Sarah's tennis racket, leaning against the wall.

Iris took half a step into the closet. She whispered, "Sarah?"

There wasn't an answer, which didn't surprise Iris, after the failure with the recorder, but still she felt less alone. Like Sarah was listening, even if she couldn't answer.

"I got you a present," Iris said. She paused for a minute, unsure what to do with the ribbon-wrapped book. Then she knelt and placed it on the floor next to the tennis racket. She could still hear her parents' voices, laughing as they argued over the best way to load the dishwasher.

Iris blinked into the closet's darkness.

She thought about it all again. She remembered how they'd stood there together, near the edge of the schoolyard, waiting for Sarah's mom to pick them up. Iris had been leaning against the fence; Sarah had been closer to the curb.

It was a fine day, like all days were—a big blue sky, salty fresh air, a breeze that wasn't cold and seemed to whisper that summer would be coming soon.

Alison Fredricks and her mom drove by, honking cheerfully and waving. Their windows were rolled down.

It had been a Friday. The weekend was there, and Sarah and Iris had been making plans.

"Let's stay at your place," Sarah said. "My mom is making that awful meatloaf tonight."

And those were the last words Iris ever heard Sarah say.

Because then the car came around the corner, too fast, and not in its own lane, black like a shadow but not harmless like one. And there had been a scream that sounded like a person, except maybe it had been a car's brakes— stepped on hard, but not *that* car's, because later the police would say that it hadn't even slowed down. The hood of the car had scooped Sarah up like she was made of stuffing or straw, like she didn't weigh anything at all.

At the hospital the police officer told Iris's parents,

"It's a miracle that your girl is okay. Not even a scratch. Someone up there must have been looking out for her today."

But if that was true—if it *was* a miracle that Iris was unharmed, if someone "up there" *had* been looking out for her, then what did it mean that Sarah was the opposite of unharmed? That Sarah was dead?

No matter how many times she thought about it, Iris couldn't see how it made any sense.

Right then, kneeling in the hall closet, the hanging coats swaying around her like mourners, Iris wanted nothing more than to see Sarah step forward and pick up the book. She wanted it so strongly, so completely, that it seemed as if it must happen, as if it *would* surely happen if only she waited long enough, believed deeply enough. But it didn't happen. And at last she stood, and sighed. "Happy Birthday," she whispered. She stepped back out and shut the door.

Winter was long and deep. It snowed a few times, but mostly it rained, and the rain turned the occasional snow to slush. By the middle of March, it had warmed enough that Iris's mom said she could ride the bus to school again, and Iris's dad started to get busy preparing for his garden.

He'd spent the winter sitting at the kitchen table with a cup of coffee and a rotating pile of gardening books that he'd checked out of the library. He'd taken three more trips to his favorite gardening supply store in Portland and had started following half a dozen gardening blogs.

One of his favorite books was all about identifying and eliminating common soil pests, and about the natural enemies of pests—the good bugs that would prey on the bad bugs. It was full of close-up photographs of beetles, wasps, and flies. Iris found it hard to believe that a fly could ever be a good thing. Her favorite was the assassin bug. It was mostly green with yellow and black stripes down its sides.

"We're going to feast this summer," Iris's dad said a lot, flipping through his books, tracing a finger along a plump red tomato, a spiny zucchini leaf.

But it was too soon, and too wet, for him to put anything in the ground, so in between preparing the soil with various nutrients and fertilizers, Iris's dad occupied himself with plans—for the garden, and for springtime's flock of chickens. "Orpingtons are probably the way to go," Iris heard him tell her mother for maybe the fifteenth time. "They're gentle, they lay lots of eggs, and they're good-looking chickens too."

This last part made Iris's mom laugh. "Does it matter what they look like?" she asked. "We're going to eat their eggs, not take them to the prom."

"They might as well look good," said her dad. "A healthy flock can be yard art. A pleasure to see through the kitchen window in the morning."

He'd reserved an incubator for them to rent. And he told Iris that she could be in charge of naming "the girls."

"We're going to have at least half a dozen hens," he told her. "That way when they start laying, we'll have plenty of eggs for us, and some to give away to friends. I'll bet Katherine McBride wouldn't say no to a freshly laid dozen eggs every now and again."

Her dad whistled a lot lately. Along with his gardening books, he had gathered a collection of titles like *Living Off the Grid* and *A Biosustainable You.* One day when Iris came home from school, her dad was out back, setting up a tumbling composter. "Check this out, Pigeon," he said.

The composter was a black plastic octagon raised

up on triangular legs that let it spin freely. "We just put our kitchen scraps in here," her dad told her, "and we rotate it every couple of days, like this." He grabbed the handholds and gave the composter a spin. "In a couple of weeks, finished compost will be ready for our garden. And the whole thing is rodent-proof." He beamed a smile at her.

Iris imagined a swarm of rats trying to breech the composter, unable to get in. "Great, Dad," she said.

Iris's mom was busy too, and at the dinner table she told them about her research. A grant proposal she'd written with one of her colleagues had been approved, and she was working on a new project. "Betty and I are looking into defensins," she reported over a bowl of beef stew.

"Is that a real word?" Iris asked.

"Sure is," said her mom. "Defensins are manufactured by the body. They're naturally occurring antimicrobial peptides."

"Slow down, Professor," said Iris's dad.

Her mom laughed. "That's a fancy way of saying that they are the first line of defense against infection. But some people don't seem to make enough of them. That might be why some people get sick, and other people don't. We're trying to learn more."

Could the unfairness of who got sick and who didn't really be explained? Iris wondered.

And Iris herself was busy. There was homework, of course, and caring for Charles, and more afternoons spent with Boris. Iris still didn't *love* Magic. But it was something she and Boris could do in the rain. And there were some things she liked about it.

She liked that when she played Magic, she became a Planeswalker—a magician with the ability to walk from one plane of existence to another. And she liked the game's balance between preparedness and uncertainty.

Boris taught her how to build her own deck, balancing Land cards and Spell cards. Iris liked that she could build her deck any way she wanted, and she liked that after she shuffled it, there was no way to know which seven cards she would draw.

Most of all, she liked being in charge of a world. Even if she lost a game, she could look back at the cards in her graveyard and see where mistakes had been made.

And then she could reshuffle her deck, reanimating everything that had died, and challenge Boris to a rematch.

They were dealing out their cards for a third game one rainy afternoon, a tray of snacks and cocoa off to one side. They sat on the floor of Boris's bedroom. He and his sisters had gotten a puppy a few weeks earlier, a velvety black spaniel named Flora, who lay sprawled above them on Boris's bed, gnawing determinedly on one of Charlotte's slippers.

"Your dog is pretty cute," Iris admitted.

"She'd be a lot cuter if she hadn't chewed the corner off my Liliana," Boris said.

"You can still use the card," Iris said for the fourth time.

"But its resale value," he moaned.

They took turns rolling the die. Boris rolled a two; Iris rolled a six, so she got to choose who went first.

"You go," she said.

They fell into their game, and didn't talk about much other than the cards in front of them. That was something else Iris liked about Magic—when they were playing, everything else sort of went away.

It didn't bother Iris when Boris beat her again. She'd

won only a few times, but Boris never took it easy on her, so when she did occasionally win, she knew it counted.

"You should consider incorporating some red cards into your deck," Boris advised as they cleaned up.

"I'll think about it," Iris said.

She heard the doorbell ring. "Gotta go." She snapped a rubber band around her deck and shoved it into her backpack.

"See ya," answered Boris. He was carefully stacking his cards and sliding them into the deck box. Flora lay stretched out on the bed, fast asleep. She'd worn herself out with all the slipper chewing.

It had been a while since Iris and Boris had talked about their list, since they'd tried to contact Sarah. After the EVP failure, Boris seemed to want to avoid the whole thing. Iris figured it had made him really uncomfortable, watching her cry like that, and listening to all that silence they'd recorded.

But Iris hadn't forgotten about her desire to speak with Sarah, and she hadn't forgotten, either, about Boris's miracle.

"Hey," said Iris, before she left the room. She tried to make her voice sound casual, like this wasn't something she'd been thinking too much about. "Didn't you say the Vatican would be visiting in the spring? To check out your miracle?"

"Uh-huh. Next month, I think."

"So, do you think . . . I mean, would it be okay if I came over that day?" Iris felt nervous, worried that Boris might think this was a weird request.

Boris looked up. "You want to be here when the Vatican visits?"

Iris shrugged. "I guess. I mean, yeah. If it's okay."

"It's going to be really boring," he warned.

"That's okay with me." Iris held her breath, waiting for Boris to answer.

Boris blinked. "I guess," he said. "Maybe you could ask them . . . you know, about the miracle thing."

Iris smiled. "Really?" she said. "You wouldn't mind?"

"Why would I mind?" asked Boris. "We're friends, aren't we?"

That night when Iris got home, she found her dad setting up the incubator in the living room. Charles was curled up on the hearth in his usual spot, watching him.

The incubator was about the size and shape of a mini-fridge. It was silver, stainless steel, with a large rectangular window in the front. A set of digital numbers flashed across the top, next to the words ReptiPro 6000.

"This baby's got two automatic egg turners," her dad said, patting the top of the incubator and grinning at Iris and her mom. "It'll turn the eggs six times a day. It's got a fan to circulate the air, and it's got this light you can switch on to check on the eggs. It's got a highly accurate digital display. It's top of the line."

Iris's mom snorted a little, like she was trying not to laugh. "Great, Frank," she said. "We're all set, then."

"We're going to have the healthiest flock of chickens in the valley," he said, ignoring her.

"Umm . . ." Iris looked around the room. "So, where are the eggs?"

"They'll be here in seven to ten days," her dad said. "I ordered Buff Orpingtons from a farm up near Astoria."

"How long will it take them to hatch?" asked Iris's mom.

"About three weeks."

"Well," said her mom, "I guess you'd better get busy on that coop."

"It's not that big of a rush," said her dad. "The chicks will have to live inside for at least a month."

"*Excuse* me?" said her mom. "What was that?"

"Oh, yeah," said her dad. "Four weeks, maybe six. Don't worry. I'll build them a playpen in the kitchen."

He patted the top of the incubator once more, and then headed, whistling, to check on dinner.

17

The eggs arrived exactly a week later. A dozen of them, just like a dozen eggs you'd buy at the store, all light brown, all perfect.

Iris's dad was beside himself with excitement. Very carefully, one at a time, he transferred the eggs from the shipping container to the incubator.

"If we're lucky," he said, "eight or ten of these eggs will hatch. If we're really lucky, at least half of them will be pullets—girl chickens."

"What'll we do with the boys?" Iris asked. "We're not eating them."

"No, no, we already talked about that," her dad

assured her. "I met a couple of guys in town, at the hardware store. They have a bigger farm not too far from here, and when I told them about our plans, after they stopped laughing at me and calling us "city folk," they offered to take any cockerels we hatch."

Iris was suspicious. "Are *they* going to eat them?"

"I made them promise they wouldn't." Her dad shut and latched the incubator door. "They breed chickens for egg laying and shipping, and they said they could use some new studs for their flock."

That sounded okay to Iris. "So we'll end up with, like, four chickens?"

"Maybe more," said her dad. "Think positive."

He pressed a couple of buttons on the front of the incubator. It started humming, and the temperature readout on the digital display began to rise.

Iris's dad had big chicken-coop plans. He wanted to make it look like a miniature version of the homestead, with a front porch and dormer windows and everything. Iris teased him that he'd have to set up a mini-composter by its back door, and a mini–wind turbine too.

He bought a chicken-coop blueprint off the Internet and then spent several evenings modifying it to more closely mimic the house.

"What do you think, Pigeon?" he asked one night after he'd spent hours poring over his work.

Iris had been sitting across from him, doing her math homework. She looked at his plans, but they didn't seem to make much sense from that upside-down angle, so she got up and went around to her father's side of the table.

Right-side up, the blueprints still didn't make any sense. "Is that how you open the coop?" she asked, pointing.

"That's the ramp," he answered. "So the chickens can get inside. To open the coop, see, there are these hinges and the roof flips open."

"Oh, yeah, I see now," said Iris. She didn't.

"Maybe I should make a few more modifications," he muttered.

The next day when Iris made her way up the driveway after the bus had dropped her off, she heard a pounding sound from around the back of the house. It wasn't raining hard, just a steady drizzle, so Iris detoured from the gravel driveway and followed the noise.

She found her dad on the back porch, surrounded by lengths of wood and boxes of shingles and nails. He was hammering together what looked to be two of the walls of the coop. He held a line of nails between his lips, and his expression was one of deep concentration— furrowed brow, tightened jaw, narrowed eyes.

"Hey, Dad," Iris said. "How's it going?"

"Grmlph," he answered.

"Huh," Iris said. "You want something to drink?"

"Coffee," he said, or at least that's what Iris figured he said. Coffee was his answer to most questions.

Charles was curled in a blanket on the center of the kitchen table. Only the tips of his ears stuck out. Iris pulled the blanket up a little, to cover them.

She spooned coffee grounds into the filter and filled the coffeemaker with water. Then she flipped the switch to "On" and sat at the table to wait for the coffee to be done.

"How was your day, Charles?"

The lump on the table didn't make a sound.

The coffee brewed. Its warm, nutty scent filled the kitchen.

The lump began to move. Ears emerged, and then a nose.

"It's like you're a heat magnet, Charles," said Iris, and she scooped him up and plopped him onto her lap, blanket and all.

When the coffee was done, Iris placed Charles on her chair, tucking him in again. Then she got her dad's favorite mug out of the cabinet and filled it.

"Good talk, Charles," she called over her shoulder as she headed back outside.

Her dad was sitting cross-legged on the porch, staring at what he'd built. From the look of the mess of wooden slats tilting to one side, Iris guessed he must have used all the nails he'd held in his mouth, and probably most of the rest of them too. Nails stuck out at all different angles.

"How's it coming?" Iris asked.

"Not great," he answered.

Iris nodded. She handed him his mug.

He took a sip. "Good coffee."

They sat together for a while, watching the walls of the chicken coop list farther to one side. At last Iris said, "Maybe a simpler design?"

"You think?" Her dad sighed and ran his fingers through his hair.

"Maybe we shouldn't have moved here," Iris said. Her voice was quiet, and she wondered if her dad hadn't heard her. But then he reached over and squeezed her hand.

"You miss California?" he asked.

Iris shrugged. "I miss some things," she said. "I miss the ocean." *I miss Sarah,* she thought.

"I miss things too," said her dad. "But there's lots of good stuff here. Like Boris. Like this house. And the eggs. I can't wait to see how many hatch."

"Mom's job is good too, right?"

"Mm-hmm. She's in her element."

"And you don't mind being home all the time?"

"I love it," said her dad. "Even on days like this, when I discover I'm no chicken-coop contractor."

"Don't be so hard on yourself, Dad. You're good at lots of things."

"Thanks, Pigeon," he said. "You're good at lots of things too. Making coffee, for one. Excellent coffee."

The drizzle grew heavier. They were protected from it on the back porch, and they watched together as it swelled into rain. It had been half a year now that Iris and her parents had lived in Oregon, and in that time Iris had learned a lot about rain—its transition from soft to hard, the various sounds of it against the roof, the way it could mist and float and softly fill the air, the way it could pound the earth with bulletlike intensity.

In Oregon, the question was never *would* there be rain, but rather *what kind* of rain there would be.

"Maybe I'll buy a kit," Iris's dad mused.

"They sell kits?"

"Oh, yeah," said her dad. "The chicken-coop industry is a moneymaking machine."

"Huh," said Iris. "Yeah. Maybe a kit is a good idea."

"All right," he said. "I'll get a kit. And what about you, Pigeon?"

"Me?" said Iris. "What about me?"

"Spring's coming up," he said. "I hear your school has a tennis team. Have you given any thought to trying out?"

Iris was quiet.

"It might be good for you, Pigeon. You were getting pretty good before . . . before we moved."

Iris knew what he had been about to say. Before Sarah died. And it wasn't even all that true. She was never really good at tennis. Not good like Sarah was. Iris liked playing, that was true, but it was more because she liked being with her friend than because of the actual sport.

She liked the funny little sound Sarah made when she scored a point. She liked the perfect *thump* of the tennis ball when it hit the sweet spot of Sarah's racket. She liked watching Sarah double-knot her shoes. She liked the *idea* of tennis, that even if you have nothing—not a single point—you still have Love.

"I can't play tennis here—there's too much rain," she muttered. "I'd better go do my homework. I have to write a paper about what it means to be a good citizen."

"Huh," said her dad. "That sounds pretty boring."

Iris laughed a little. "Yeah."

"Well, let me know if you need any ideas," her dad offered.

"Okay. Let me know if you need any help with the coop."

Inside, Iris found that Charles had abandoned his fluffy blue blanket. He was in the living room, spread out across the top of the incubator like it was a tanning bed. His tail was unfurled, limp. He seemed to be smiling.

Maybe they should keep the incubator, Iris thought, after the eggs were hatched. For Charles. She stroked his head, and he twitched a little.

Then she knelt down and stared into the incubator, at the eggs. All twelve eggs lay perfectly still in their individual grooves.

She thought of the eggs, the way her dad had all these hopes and plans for them. She thought of him, out on the porch with his tilting, awful chicken-coop project. She thought of how her parents had moved her here, far from home, far from her memories.

She thought about Sarah's tennis racket, tucked in their closet. Iris remembered when Sarah had gotten the racket as a Christmas present from her parents two years ago.

Sarah had laughed, telling Iris about how it had been wrapped. "They didn't box it up or anything," she said. "They just stuck a big gold bow right in the center of its head."

Iris thought of all the things Sarah's parents had hoped for that racket. They'd probably wanted Sarah to use it on the junior high school tennis team. Maybe they thought she'd win some trophies with it. Maybe they figured that she'd use it to teach her younger sister and brother how to play tennis, even.

One thing Iris knew. There was no way Sarah's parents ever could have guessed that their Christmas present would end up here, in the middle of Oregon, a thousand miles away from where they'd tucked it under a Christmas tree.

And yet here it was. Here *she* was.

You can make your plans, Iris thought. *You can shelter your eggs, and keep them warm and dry. But even still. Even still.*

18

On the eighth of April, Boris passed Iris a note during Social Studies. They were in the middle of playing a geography game called Where in the World. The teacher had told them to break into two teams, and Heather had asked Iris to be on hers.

Iris couldn't help but feel suspicious of Heather. Was she just being nice to Iris because she felt sorry for her, because Iris had a dead friend and hung out with Boris every day at lunch?

Iris didn't like the way the other kids acted with Boris—they didn't pay any attention to him half the time, and when they did, it was usually to make fun of him. Not in a really *mean* way, not threatening or bullying, just sort of messing with him. Like there was nothing better to do.

So being his friend meant that Iris got mostly ignored, and occasionally teased, too. Never anything terrible, but nothing really great. Heather, though, seemed to want to be friends. She kept being friendly, even though Iris hadn't been. Like today, asking Iris to be on her team. She didn't *have* to do that.

Boris was on the other team, so when he passed Iris the note, everyone on his team mumbled accusations that he was giving Iris answers because he *Liked* her.

"People can be stupid," Heather said knowingly, and Iris realized that even though most of the other kids had, Heather had never once made fun of Boris.

So she smiled at Heather and shrugged, hands up, like, *What can you do?* And they both laughed.

Iris didn't open the note until the bell rang and the class rumbled into movement, gathering books, coats, backpacks. Heather lingered near the door like maybe she was waiting for Iris, but after a minute she went out into the hallway.

Maybe it would be okay to have another friend, Iris thought.

The note read, *Vatican at my house today! Want to come over after school?*

The message left Iris feeling queasy and excited for the rest of the afternoon.

She peppered Boris with questions during lunch— "How many people are visiting? What do they look like? Are you sure they'll still be there this afternoon?"

Boris didn't have answers to the first two questions, since they were due to arrive after he'd left for school. But he answered her third question confidently—"Of *course* they'll still be there. They're here to meet *me*. I'm the miracle, after all."

Boris was the miracle. That was almost impossible to believe, sitting across from him, watching him eat spoonfuls of macaroni and cheese.

There was nothing miraculous about the way Boris ate. Most days, it was all Iris could do to ignore his chew-talk.

But still, he was the miracle.

"I'll call my dad from your place and tell him I'll need him to pick me up after dinner," Iris said.

When Boris and Iris came in through the kitchen door, dripping wet as usual, there were four people in Boris's kitchen. Katherine was there, wearing makeup and a blouse Iris had never seen her in before. She was sitting at the table along with three men, surrounded by stacks of papers and spilling file folders. When Boris and Iris walked in, the men stood up, all with broad smiles. Two of the men were priests. They wore long black robes with short black collars. Each priest's collar had a notch in the front that showed a square of the white band underneath.

The third man was dressed in a suit. It was a very nice suit, Iris thought, as far as suits went. It was dark gray with light gray pinstripes. This man wore a wide red tie and had a square of red silk tucked into his jacket pocket. All three men wore glasses.

One of the priests was very old, and tall, and thin, with wispy white hair combed across his half-bald scalp. The other priest was younger, and fatter, and he had all of his hair.

The man in the suit was younger than the old priest but older than the young one. He wasn't fat or thin, and though he was balding, he was just losing the hair at his temples, not on the top of his head.

The young priest said something in Italian, and the man in the suit nodded.

"Boris, there you are," said Katherine. "Hello, Iris. Nice to see you, honey."

"Hi, Katherine," said Iris. She couldn't take her eyes off the old, white-haired priest. His eyes were liquid blue behind the round wire frames of his glasses, and he stared without blinking at Boris.

Nothing about the men struck Iris as particularly magical or powerful, and Iris felt a pricking of disappointment.

"Boris, Iris," said Katherine, "this is Monsignor Augustin, Father Santorno, and Mr. Gardello. Gentlemen, this is my son, Boris, and his friend Iris."

The three visitors smiled and nodded politely at Iris, but really they only had eyes for Boris.

"It is our great pleasure to meet you," said the young priest, Father Santorno, who seemed to be speaking on behalf of all three of them.

"It's nice to meet you, too," said Boris, who looked, Iris thought, distinctly uncomfortable.

Boris held out his hand, and each of the three men shook it, first the man in the suit, then the young priest, then the older one. He held Boris's hand for a long time, patting it with his other hand, and examining Boris's face.

When he finally let go of Boris's hand, he grasped Boris's cheeks and kissed him on the top of his head. Then he lifted his glasses and wiped his eyes.

Boris cleared his throat, shifted his weight from foot to foot.

"We're going to be a while longer, going through all this paperwork," said Katherine, clearly giving Boris permission to leave the room. "We'll call you in when we're done, all right?"

"Sure!" said Boris, grinning with relief. "Come on, Iris. Let's go play . . . cards for a while."

Iris noticed that Boris didn't say "Magic."

"Actually," she said, "do you mind, Katherine, if I hang out in here and watch?"

"You want to watch us go through all these medical files?" Katherine's tone was incredulous.

"Uh-huh. If that's okay."

Katherine looked at the men standing around the table. They were all politely waiting, each with a folder open in front of him.

"Sure. Why not?" said Katherine.

Boris rolled his eyes. "Whatever," he said. "I'll be in my room if you get bored. *When* you get bored." He waved at the three men. "Nice to meet you," he said again, but the way he retreated hastily from the kitchen made it seem like he didn't think it was very nice at all.

The young priest, Father Santorno, offered Iris his seat. "Oh, no, that's okay," she said. She grabbed the yellow stool from the corner by the phone and swung it around, wedging it next to Katherine's chair.

Then it was as if she became invisible. The men sat back down, turned their attention to the files in front of them, and Iris listened as they asked Katherine question after question.

Most of them were medical—"At what point during the pregnancy did you first learn that there was an irregularity with the child?"

"Twenty-four weeks," said Katherine.

"At that time, what was the amniotic fluid level?"

"Less than one. Fifteen is considered average; less than four is critical."

"What did the doctors suspect caused the problem?"

"Either a genetic abnormality, a chromosomal abnormality, or a virus."

"What were the results of the unborn baby's B2 test?"

"Very disheartening. They found that his kidneys were

extremely damaged. They told us that ninety to ninety-five percent of babies born with kidney function like our baby's die shortly after birth."

The two priests nodded and smiled at this response, and the older priest said something in Italian. Father Santorno scratched a note in his folder.

"And even if his kidneys proved to be healthy after birth, the baby still faced many difficult hurdles, yes?" This question came from the man in the suit, Mr. Gardello.

"Yes," answered Katherine. "There was a strong likelihood that Boris's lungs had been damaged, as a result of my low amniotic fluid level. If his lungs failed to develop, there would be nothing anyone could do for him when he was born. The doctors warned us that when he tried to breathe for the first time, or when the doctors attempted to resuscitate him, it was probable that his lungs would just crack, break, and fall apart."

"But that didn't happen."

"No," said Katherine. "That didn't happen."

"Your son's name—Boris—that is an unusual name for an American boy, no?"

"Yes," said Katherine. "It is. Originally, we had planned to name him Andrew. After my husband's father. But when we got the news about his condition—about all the hurdles he'd have to jump just to stay alive—we decided he needed another name. A fighting name. Boris means 'one who fights for glory.' It seemed appropriate."

"Yes," said Father Santorno. "Very."

"And the nuns," said the Monsignor. His accent was heavy. "They prayed for the boy. They prayed that Pope Paul would save him."

Katherine shifted in her seat, as if the question made her uncomfortable. "That's what my cousin says," she answered. Then she said, "Look, I'm happy to help you out. It's important to my cousin that I do. But I'm not the right person to speak with about the nuns, or the pope they're hoping to have sainted. The way I see it, we were incredibly lucky. We beat the odds. If anyone worked any miracles, it was Boris, in healing himself. And of course the doctors who performed the surgeries Boris needed during the first couple of years of his life. And the ultrasound technician who found what was wrong with the baby in the first place. Even after healing himself and surviving, without modern medicine, Boris would have been in a terrible pickle. Modern medicine, and a healthy dose of good luck."

Iris looked at the priests to see their reaction. Would they be mad at Katherine for doubting that Boris's survival was a miracle? She couldn't help but wonder if maybe, by saying those words—that it was the *doctors* who helped Boris, along with luck—that the priests or God Himself could be angered, could decide to take the miracle back. She half listened for the sound of Boris's body falling instantly dead.

But the men didn't seem upset. Their benign facial expressions didn't change, and none of them raised his voice. Father Santorno even smiled a little before he said, "God works in mysterious ways."

"That may be," said Katherine, rising and stretching her back. "Can I offer you gentlemen a cup of tea? I'm absolutely parched."

Tea sounded good to all the visitors, and they spoke to each other in quiet, melodic Italian while Katherine filled the kettle and lit a flame beneath it.

Monsignor Augustin asked something, and Mr. Gardello flipped through a file, found an ultrasound image of Boris before he was born, and handed it across the table to him.

Iris looked at the picture. Curled in upon himself, his bones exposed, his head too large for his body, Boris as a fetus could have been a seedpod, a hairless cat, a chick inside an egg. He could have been anything.

Katherine pulled some cookies from a bin in the pantry and arranged them on a plate. When the water boiled, she poured it over black tea leaves in a cheery red ceramic pot. The men pulled together the papers strewn across the table, tapped them into piles, and set them aside to make room for the cups and plates. Katherine set out five of everything, and asked Iris to pour the tea.

It seemed to Iris that she wouldn't get a better chance than this, when the priests' attention was on the cookies and tea rather than the documents and pictures. So after she poured the tea, Iris cleared her throat. "Excuse me. Father? Monsignor?" She wasn't Catholic; the terms felt funny in her mouth. But she forged ahead. "Can I ask you something?"

Father Santorno was the one to answer. He smiled kindly and said, "Of course. What is your question?"

Now that she was here, finally, Iris had a hard time forming her question—the one she'd been thinking about since Boris had told her about his miracle. The one, actually, that she'd been pondering even longer than that, since last spring. "I just wanted to know," she said, "if Boris's recovery was a miracle . . . You *do* think it was a miracle, right?"

"Most certainly," said Father Santorno. "I have been through his files very carefully. I have spoken with all his doctors. I have corresponded with the fine sisters who prayed to Pope Paul. It seems clear to me that if not for the hand of God, Boris would not have survived."

The other two men nodded in agreement.

"Okay," said Iris. "But . . . why Boris?"

"What do you mean, child?"

"I mean, why Boris? Why should *he* get a miracle? Not that I wish he didn't, or anything. Of course I'm glad he's alive. But don't you ever wonder how God decides who gets the miracles? And why doesn't *everyone* get a miracle, if miracles are real? If God is real? I mean, if I had the power to make good things happen, and to stop bad things from happening, I wouldn't just do it for some people. I'd want to help everyone. All the time."

Iris was crying. Her nose was running, and she rubbed her sleeve angrily across her face. She hadn't meant to cry. She just wanted to ask her question, the same question she'd asked Dr. Shannon, the same question she'd asked herself over and over again. Why Boris? Why her? And why not Sarah?

Katherine, sitting back down, squeezed her shoulder. She looked at the men from the Vatican as though she, too, would very much like to hear the answer.

Father Santorno handed Iris a napkin. He said, "The questions you ask, child, are good questions. They are questions each of us asks, many times."

Iris took a ragged breath. She picked up a cookie, just to have something to do with her hands. "Well," she said, "what's the answer?"

"The answer," said Father Santorno, "is faith. Faith that God has heard us—that He always hears us. And that if it seems that He does not answer, it may rather be that He has not answered in the way we would like. We must have faith that His answer is the right one, even if we cannot see why, or how."

Iris took a bite of her cookie. She didn't want to be

rude, but it seemed to her that Father Santorno's response was the worst answer she had ever heard.

She looked over at Katherine. "I think I'll go play some Magic with Boris," she said.

She pushed back from the table and left the kitchen. Behind her, she heard the three men begin their interrogation again.

19

April was almost half over before the ground finally warmed up enough for Iris's dad to plant his garden. He had a soil thermometer that he'd stuck into the ground, in the turned-over dirt that was going to be the garden. It looked just like the meat thermometer they kept in the utensil drawer, except bigger.

Finally, on a Sunday afternoon, Iris's dad came whistling into the kitchen carrying the soil thermometer, its long metal spike coated with black dirt. "Today's the day," he sang. "Soil temperature has held steady just above sixty degrees since Tuesday. It's planting day!"

Iris was at the table, eating a bowl of cereal and flipping through a graphic novel Boris had loaned her. He had raved about how great it was, but Iris thought it was kind of stupid.

The story was about a boy named Harvey who had a superpower that let him turn into any animal, anytime. That part was okay, but the animals he chose to morph into seemed predictable. She was on page thirty-one, and so far he'd become a snake, a spider, and a great white shark.

If it had been her, Iris would have come up with better animals to become. Right off the top of her head she thought of a narwhal and a flying squirrel. When her dad came in through the kitchen door, Iris was considering whether it would be possible to become an extinct animal, like a dodo bird—something that didn't exist anymore, something that would never live again.

"Put on your mud boots," said her dad. "I'm going to need your help."

Iris looked out the big window above the sink. The sky was as gray as ever; a fine mist floated in the air. "It's raining," she said, and turned back to her book.

Her dad walked over and looked down at her. Iris could *feel* him looking at her. She ignored him. He reached out, took hold of her book, and pulled it from her hands. He closed it.

"Hey!" said Iris. "You lost my spot!"

"Pigeon," he said, sliding into the seat across from her, "if we wait for the rain to go away, we might never plant our garden."

"Well, I can't help it if it's stupid here," Iris said.

Her dad sighed. "There is lot of rain. But Pigeon, let's not let the rain dictate our lives."

Iris wanted to shake her father. "You want me to just *ignore* the rain?"

"No," he said. "I don't expect you to ignore it. You *can't* ignore it—nearly every day is a rainy day. But I want you to learn to live with the rain. To live *in* it. Eventually, it will fade into the background, little by little. I promise you. But you've got to make plans, to plant gardens, to go outside. In spite of the rain. Even if you get wet."

Iris had the feeling her dad wasn't just talking about the rain.

Iris's mom came in from the living room. Her glasses were on top of her head, and her hair was kind of wild, the way it got when she was working on a problem. Like the energy from her brain frizzed her hair.

Charles was at her heels. He looked pleased with himself, and very dapper.

Iris couldn't help laughing. "What is *that?*" she asked. Charles was wearing a blue and yellow striped turtleneck sweater. It looked like something her father would wear, except shrunk down. And he crossed the kitchen proudly, his tail waving high in the air as if to announce his arrival. Weaving through the legs of the kitchen table, he purred.

"You like it?" asked Iris's mom. "I ordered it online."

Charles leaped onto Iris's lap and circled, stretched his claws, lay down.

"He looks kind of ridiculous," said Iris, "but he seems warmer." She rubbed his side through the sweater.

"I think he likes it," said her mom.

"Very handsome, Charles," said Iris's dad. Then he told her mom, "Guess what? The ground is warm again today."

"Time to plant the garden?"

He nodded, scratched his beard. "Today's the day."

"I'll get my boots," Iris's mom said.

Her dad put the thermometer in the sink and poured a cup of coffee. "I'll be outside," he said. Before he opened the door, he flipped up the hood of his jacket. "Button up, Pigeon," he said. "It's cold out there." Then he winked and headed out to the garden.

A minute later, Iris heard her mother's booted footsteps as she reentered the kitchen.

"Iris?" she said. "I found something in the hall closet. Is this yours?"

Iris knew before she looked up what her mother would be holding. There it was—the ribbon-wrapped copy of *Anne of Green Gables*. Iris flushed. "I guess so," she said.

Her mom walked over to the table, pulled a chair close to Iris's, and sat down. Her flowered raincoat created a bright spot in the kitchen. Iris didn't look right at her, but in the edge of her vision she saw the way all the colors melted together—purple and red and yellow and pink. Like a spring bouquet.

"What was it doing in the closet?" asked her mom.

She shouldn't feel embarrassed, Iris told herself. But she did. "I got it for Sarah," she mumbled. Beneath her hand, Charles stretched a little, settled further into sleep.

Her mother stroked Iris's hair. For a minute she was

quiet. Then she asked, "Sarah loved this book, didn't she?"

Iris felt that she had as little control over her tears as she did the drops that fell from the sky.

"It was her favorite."

"May I?" asked her mother. Her fingers were poised to loosen the ribbon.

Miserably, Iris nodded. She watched as her mother pulled the end of the red and white bow, watched as the first loop slipped free, as the bow flattened into a line. Her mom undid the knot and set the ribbon aside. She opened the cover and flipped through the pages. The edges were gilt, and they shone under the kitchen light.

"I loved this book when I was a girl," said her mom. "I loved Anne's great big imagination."

"So did Sarah," Iris said.

"Remember that scene, when Anne is walking with Diana through the woods after she fell off the ridgepole of the roof and sprained her ankle?"

"Uh-huh."

"And remember how she was telling Diana that ghost story, and she thought that the woods were haunted?"

Iris remembered.

"And then she fell down. Didn't she trip on some-thing?"

"She walked over an old boarded-up well. She broke through the wood and got stuck. Diana had to leave her there to go get help."

"That's right! I'd forgotten that she got stuck. And then she got herself so worked up and scared that she actually *fainted*. Isn't that what happened?"

Iris nodded.

Her mom flipped through the book some more. Finally she said, "Pigeon? Why was the book in the closet?"

The words came out in a whisper. "It was for Sarah's birthday."

"Oh," said her mother. "And that's where you think Sarah is? In the closet under the stairs?"

Iris shrugged. It sounded ridiculous, when her mother said it like that. She braced herself for what her mother would say next—that there was no such thing as ghosts, that Sarah wasn't in their house, that Sarah was gone and wasn't coming back.

She didn't want to hear her mom say this. And if she did, Iris was ready to argue—her mom couldn't *prove* that Sarah wasn't there in the house, in the closet.

Miracles could happen, after all. Claude said she could communicate with ghosts, and all those people online who believed in EVP, they believed that the dead weren't all-the-way gone. And look at Boris—look at what had happened to him. That was a miracle; it had been studied, examined by those priests, researched for hours, and they gave it their stamp of approval. And didn't they know more about what was possible—what miracles might occur—than Iris's mother?

But her mother didn't try to convince Iris that she was wrong, or that Sarah wasn't in their closet. All she said was, "I'll bet Sarah would love it if you'd keep this beautiful book up in your room, on the shelf with all your other books. I'll bet she'd want you to read it. To enjoy it enough for the both of you. Do you think you can do that?" She closed the book and slid it across the table, to Iris.

Iris traced the picture of the two girls on the cover. The two best friends. She took a deep breath, and she nodded.

"Good," said her mother, standing and fastening the belt of her raincoat. "Then what do you say we go play in the mud with your dad?"

* * *

Iris didn't think she had ever seen her dad so happy. He'd tucked his mud-splattered khaki pants into his rain boots, and he was troweling rows into the rich, dark soil of his garden patch.

"Grab a shovel!" he called to Iris when she stomped down the back stairs and through the yard. Mist still floated across the grass, and everywhere Iris looked was wet. She hoisted a shovel and started turning the dirt at the far end of the garden, mixing in the coffee grounds and organic fertilizer her dad had poured over it.

Each turn of the spade revealed life—plump pink worms, wiggling blindly, tiny hairlike roots from plants that had once grown. Gray-brown mushrooms, thick-headed and thin-spined, that sliced easily when Iris pressed into them with the side of her shovel.

The dirt smelled *good*—wet and strong and familiar. And Iris remembered sitting on the floor of their Seal Beach home, digging through the dirt in their potted plants. Now, working in the garden, it was as if she was carried back to that time.

Her mother was on her knees in a rocky patch of the garden, sifting the dirt through her fingers and separating out pebbles. She was humming.

Iris had listened to her dad talk about his plans all winter long, so she knew what they would be planting, and where: chives, parsley, and radishes in the bed closest to the house; carrots, beets, broccoli, and leeks in the raised planter just a little farther; and Brussels sprouts, cabbage, cauliflower, lettuce, peas, rhubarb, and spinach out near the far edge of the garden.

All of the plants would be surrounded by a fence her father was to erect next month, before the chickens were big enough to be outside. Today they were still nestled in their shells, though according to her dad's calendar, they were due to hatch in three or four more days.

Eventually, the hens would have their own coop on the other side of the house, but Iris's dad wanted them to free-range on the lawn a few hours a day, and he didn't want them to be able to get to the vegetables.

"Healthy chickens need access to worms and bugs," he had said, and when Iris told him that was disgusting, he said, "It's worms and bugs that make eggs taste so good!"

Iris couldn't tell whether or not he was joking.

But working in the garden—turning the soil, helping her dad trowel the rows, and later, pouring out the seeds that would one day become her family's food, carefully tucking them under the rich, dark earth—it all felt good. And even though her nose and fingers were cold, even though the mist thickened and turned again inevitably to rain, the core of Iris, her heart, felt warm and happy.

20

The next day at school, playing Magic with Boris in the library after they'd finished their lunch, Iris asked, "Hey, Boris. Can you play this game with more than two people?"

"Sure," said Boris. "Absolutely. Actually it's better with more players. Three or four is the best, but you can have even more than that."

"Well," said Iris, "I've been thinking."

"What?"

"How about if we teach that girl Heather to play? She seems pretty nice."

Boris looked up from his cards. Blinked. "I don't think so," he said, and looked back at his hand.

"Why not?"

He shrugged. "I don't know. Isn't it okay the way it is?"

"Sure," said Iris. "But it might be fun to add someone else. You know, to make the game more interesting."

"Other kids make fun of me," Boris mumbled, so softly that Iris was only pretty sure that it was what he said.

"Not all of them," Iris answered. "I've never heard Heather make fun of you. Of anyone, I don't think."

Boris shrugged again. "I'm not that great at making friends."

"You got me to be your friend," Iris argued. "And I didn't even really want one."

Boris grinned. "We are friends, huh?"

"I guess so," said Iris. "And I could help you with making more friends. I used to be pretty good at it."

"It's not like playing cards, Iris. It's not as if there are certain rules and then you win all these friends."

"Actually," she said, "it kind of *is* like that. There are rules to making friends. Things that make it easier, anyway."

"Like what?" Boris was looking at her now. The cards in his hand drooped a little, and Iris could see their faces.

"Well, for one, like table manners. That kind of stuff matters more than you'd think, to most people."

"My table manners are fine," Boris said.

"There's room for improvement," Iris said tactfully.

Boris sighed. "That's what my mother says. Okay. Tell me when I'm doing gross stuff, all right? I'll try to be better."

"That's the spirit," said Iris. "And . . ." She wondered if she was pushing her luck, bringing up the next thing. She didn't want to hurt Boris's feelings.

"What is it?"

"Well, most kids like it when people ask them questions. You know, about their hobbies and stuff. And they don't really like it if the other person is a know-it-all."

"I can't help it if I know more than most people." Boris sounded insulted.

"Sure," said Iris, trying to make her voice soothing like Dr. Shannon's. "But you don't always have to *tell* everyone about it." She was remembering the Lego-brick conversation.

"This seems like a lot of work just for a few friends," Boris said.

"Maybe," said Iris. "But friends—the good ones—are worth the work."

"Okay," said Boris. "We'll teach Heather how to play Magic. Happy?"

Iris smiled. "I'm working on it."

My mom got Charles this striped sweater," Iris told Dr. Shannon later that afternoon. "He seems warmer."

Today Dr. Shannon was wearing jeans, but she still managed to look dressy. Her jeans were cut differently than regular jeans; they were like slacks, with pockets on the sides instead of in front, and they were a really dark blue.

She wore little leopard-print heels, too. Iris asked, pointing, "Do you wear those all day? Out in the rain and everything?"

"These?" Dr. Shannon waved her foot. "Oh, no. They'd be ruined in the rain. I wear my galoshes to the office, and then I switch into these."

"So you carry a second pair of shoes, like, in a bag, and when you get here you change?"

Dr. Shannon nodded.

"That's a lot of trouble for shoes," Iris said.

"Not really. See, I like wearing pretty shoes. It gives me pleasure. But I live in a place that isn't terribly conducive to pretty-shoe-wearing. So I adjust."

"Couldn't you just get used to wearing rain shoes all the time?"

"I suppose I *could,*" said Dr. Shannon. "But why would I want to do that?"

"It would be easier," said Iris.

"Probably. But there's more to life than easy."

Iris examined the sweater Dr. Shannon was wearing. It was purple, and kind of fuzzy, with little hairs sticking out all over the place. "I like your sweater," she said.

Dr. Shannon laughed. "Thank you," she said. "You're really into fashion today, aren't you?"

Iris shrugged. "I like that yarn," she said.

"Me too," said Dr. Shannon. "Feel it—it's so soft!" She reached over so that Iris could touch the arm of her sweater.

It *was* soft. Iris wondered if Charles would like a fuzzy sweater. "What's it made of?" she asked.

"Angora," said Dr. Shannon.

"Did you knit it?"

"Me? Oh, no. I'm not crafty like that. A friend of mine knit it for me. There's a woman in Albany, not far from here, who raises Angora rabbits and dyes the hair herself, spins it into yarn. My friend Caroline made it for me, for Hanukkah last year."

"I think maybe I'll learn how to knit," Iris said. She didn't know where the words came from, but once spoken, they sounded true.

Dr. Shannon's effusive response didn't help. "Great!" she said. "That's a great idea. Lots of people are into knitting here in Corvallis. You could take a class, or buy a book if you'd rather learn on your own."

"Maybe," said Iris.

"Well, I think it's wonderful that you're thinking of taking up a new hobby."

"Maybe," said Iris. "We'll see."

Then Dr. Shannon wanted to talk about *feelings* for a while. So they did—Iris told her about the book she'd bought for Sarah, and how she'd moved it upstairs, to her bedroom. She wasn't reading it, but she kept it on the nightstand next to her bed. Maybe, she told Dr. Shannon, she'd read it soon.

"It might be like visiting with your friend," Dr. Shannon

suggested. "Reading her favorite book, laughing over the scenes that made her laugh—it might feel like Sarah is right there with you."

Iris shrugged again. A minute passed. It wasn't uncomfortable; Iris had been visiting Dr. Shannon twice a month for a while now, and she'd gotten used to sitting quietly together. At first she'd felt like she was wasting her parents' money if she didn't fill up all the time with talking, but then her dad had told her not to worry about it, that their insurance was paying Dr. Shannon anyway, and that she could just sit without talking the whole hour, if she felt like it. And silence with Dr. Shannon was kind of nice. Dr. Shannon's gentleness made it feel safe.

After a little while, Iris said, "I've been thinking about something lately. About tennis."

"Oh?"

"Not about playing. About scoring. I've been thinking how, with tennis, when you say 'Love,' that means that you've got nothing."

"Ah," said Dr. Shannon. "Yes." She looked very interested in whatever Iris might be getting ready to say. She leaned forward, across the long orange couch, and her eyes stayed on Iris's.

"Maybe the people who made up the rules of tennis are right. But maybe they're bigger right. Like, maybe that's what *Love* means."

"You're wondering . . . if *Love* means having nothing?"

Iris nodded. "Of course, not *all* the time. Sometimes, when you love someone, it fills you up, you know? But sometimes, like if the person goes away, or if she dies, if that happens, then what? You've got nothing left. Maybe you've got *less* than nothing, even. You've got a big hole."

Dr. Shannon nodded, thoughtful, and handed Iris the box of tissues. Iris took a few, wiped her eyes. Blew her nose.

Then Dr. Shannon asked, "Do you really think that? Do you think that's true for you, with Sarah?"

"Sometimes," said Iris. "It's like I've got nothing, where Sarah used to be. Except for all this *sadness*. And all these . . . tears," she finished, tossing another tissue into the wastebasket.

Dr. Shannon waited for Iris to blow her nose again.

Then she said, "Do you know why we say 'Love' for nothing in tennis?"

Iris shook her head.

"There are different theories," Dr. Shannon said. "No one knows for sure. But some people think it's because 'Love' sounds like *'L'oeuf'*—the French word for egg. An egg is ovular, like a zero. And it's full of potential, like 'nothing' is. When you have nothing, when your egg isn't yet hatched, you don't really know what you might have, what might come from that potential."

Iris thought about that for a little while. About eggs, and nothingness, and Love.

"What happened to your friend, Iris, is a terrible thing," said Dr. Shannon. "It never should have happened. It's a real tragedy."

That was all she said. She didn't try to add a "But" sentence next, she didn't try to say something smart about life going on, or silver linings, or any of that dumb, stupid stuff that so many people tried to tell Iris, even though she didn't think they believed it themselves.

Iris appreciated that about Dr. Shannon.

* * *

A couple of days later, Iris went home with Boris after school.

"So," Iris said, finishing her shuffle and drawing seven cards, "what did the Vatican decide about your miracle? Does that guy get to be a saint, or what?" They sat cross-legged on the floor of Boris's room. Flora snored gently, curled into a ball at the foot of the bed.

"Dunno," said Boris. He was slipping into Magic mode. In a couple more minutes, he'd be practically unable to process any information other than what appeared on his cards.

"Well, did they say anything when they left?"

Boris looked up, blinked. "Huh?"

"To *you*," Iris said. "Did they say anything to you?"

"Yeah," Boris said. "Of course. They came all the way from Italy to meet me, you know."

"So what did they say?"

Boris shrugged. "I don't really know. They said some prayer, but it was in Italian. And the older guy made the sign of the cross over my head."

"Oh," said Iris. "Well, did you *feel* anything?"

"Yeah," said Boris, suddenly serious. "I did."

"What was it?" asked Iris, excited. "What did you feel?"

"Glad that they were finally leaving," Boris answered. He snorted a laugh.

Iris rolled her eyes. "Great, Boris."

"Ready to play?" he asked. "I've got a new Army of the Damned card I can't wait to use on you. It puts thirteen 2/2 Black Zombie Creature tokens onto the battlefield. I'm going to *destroy* you."

Iris wasn't surprised when Boris did, indeed, destroy her. But she *was* surprised when, while Boris was sorting his cards and putting them away, she saw a short, round basket tucked behind his Magic boxes. She had seen the basket before, but she'd never thought anything of it. Today she noticed that in it was a pile of yarn balls, one green, one red, one gold, one blue, and a set of knitting needles.

"Hey," she said. "What's that?"

"What?" said Boris. "That? That's just my knitting stuff."

"You *knit?*" said Iris.

"Course I knit," scoffed Boris. "I've got four sisters. The older two taught me how. They told me it would make me a better husband one day. I think they just wanted someone to finish their projects for them."

"Are you any good?"

"What's the point of learning how to do something if you don't get good at it?" said Boris.

Iris grinned. "Do you think you could teach me?"

"How to knit? Sure. It's not hard. Kind of boring. Repetitive. But easy, once you know the basics. What do you want to make?"

"A sweater for Charles," said Iris. "A fluffy one. Out of Angora hair."

"You want to knit a rabbit fur sweater for your hairless cat? Okay, that's pretty cool—I'll teach you."

But Iris didn't want Boris to teach her unless she had something she could teach him, too. She was tired of him always being the one who knew how to do everything.

"Listen," she said. "I want to teach *you* how to do something."

"What?" asked Boris. He sounded suspicious.

"I don't know," said Iris. "What do you want to learn? I could show you how to garden, maybe. Or how to give a hairless cat a bath."

"No, thanks," said Boris. "I think I'm better off *not* knowing how to do those things."

"Okay," said Iris. "But I'm going to teach you *something*."

"That sounds like a threat." Boris laughed. "Besides, you're already teaching me things. Like the friend stuff." He looked embarrassed for a minute, and then he said, "I invited Heather to sit with us at lunch tomorrow."

Iris felt her eyebrows shoot up in surprise. "You did? What did she say?"

Boris smiled. "She said okay," he answered. "So maybe that'll be fun, having a third player."

Iris nodded. "Maybe," she said.

That night, Iris sat in front of the fire practicing what Boris had shown her—casting on and the basic knit stitch. He'd loaned her a fat pair of needles and a ball of blue cotton yarn. Charles sat beside her, his steady gaze following the motion of the needles.

Boris was right. Knitting wasn't that hard, once you got the hang of it. And it was kind of nice to have something to do with her hands.

"Very soon," Iris told Charles, "you're going to be wearing a fuzzy hair sweater. In orange, I think."

Charles didn't answer. Something diverted his attention, and suddenly he leaped down from the hearth and headed over to the incubator. Iris unfolded her legs, set aside her knitting, and followed him.

There was a little sound, like a tiny tap. Charles's tail twitched. One of the eggs, the second one in on the bottom row, moved a little. Just the tiniest quiver. But it moved.

"Dad! Mom!" Iris ran into the kitchen. Her parents were playing gin rummy at the table. They looked up, startled.

"The eggs!"

That's all she had to say. Her dad jumped up, forgetting about the hand of cards he held. They fluttered to the kitchen floor. "It's happening," he said. He sounded like he could hardly believe it was true.

Then he rushed into the living room. Iris and her mom followed him. Charles was still there, sitting motionlessly, watching the incubator.

Now two eggs were moving—the first one and another, in the middle of the top row. And then, almost simultaneously, the chicks began to peck themselves free.

A crack emerged on the bottom egg, and it spread slowly, and then a tiny piece of shell at the center of the crack broke loose. Something tiny and light orange— "A beak," said Iris's father reverently—pecked its way through.

Then the crack widened, and the hole in the shell grew, piece by tiny piece, as the chick emerged. Above, on the top row, the second chick fought its tiny, valiant fight for freedom. Finally the first chick pushed through its head, and then its wings. The chick was damp, as if it were coming in from the rain, its feathers dark with moisture, streaked here and there with bloody mucus.

But even still, it was beautiful to Iris, and she knew her parents thought so too. All three of them gasped in unison when the little chick kicked free of its shell. It just sat there, its tiny body breathing hard, exhausted from the effort its exodus had taken.

On the top row the second chick managed to free itself, too, and then there they were, two living, breathing, perfect creatures, surrounded by all the hidden potential of the eggs around them.

Iris's dad opened the door of the incubator and very carefully scooped up one of the chicks, and then the other. He carried them over to the hearth and held them in front of the fire, warming them.

"Iris," he said. "Here. Take them."

She reached out, and her father transferred the chicks into her cupped hands. Iris could feel the beating of their hearts.

She sat on the hearth and warmed them, watching breathlessly as their feathers dried and fluffed up, and listening as they made their first little chicken sounds.

It was too much for Charles to resist, and he hopped up next to Iris on the hearth.

"Careful!" warned both of her parents, together.

"Charles is a predator," said her mom. "He can't help himself."

Iris brought the chicks closer to her chest, but Charles stepped forward, sniffing them. "Charles," she warned. "Be nice."

She opened her fingers a little to let Charles see the chicks. His ears were forward, and he didn't *look* like he wanted to eat them, so Iris lowered her hands to give him a better view.

All three of them—Iris, her father, her mother—held their breath as they waited to see what Charles would do. And then he stretched his neck forward, leaned into the chicks—and licked one of them, right on the head.

"He likes them," said Iris, triumphant. "He knows they're not food. They're family."

Charles nudged the other chick, as if prodding it to stand. It peeped.

Iris's dad shook his head. "I'll be damned," he said. "That's the craziest thing I've ever seen."

21

There weren't a lot of things Iris knew how to do that Boris would want to learn. As she knitted in the living room by the fire, she thought about what she could teach him. For the past three days, Heather had shared their lunch table. Every now and then Boris would do something gross, like rub his finger across his teeth in between bites, and Iris would kick him under the table to get him to stop.

Heather was really into horses and liked to tell them about her riding lessons out at the stable. Iris asked her, "How do you ride in all the rain?"

"There's a covered arena," Heather said. "And it's kind

of nice, listening to the rain on the roof while I ride. And since it's cold, the horse's breath comes out in big puffs of steam, like a dragon's. You can come out sometime, if you want, to watch me ride. You can help me groom the horse."

That sounded fun to Iris, but Boris said, "No way. Have you ever seen one of those things poop? Disgusting." Then Heather laughed, but not in a mean way, and then Iris laughed too, and so did Boris.

Iris liked the way the needles felt when they rubbed together. She liked the neat, tight row of stitches she was making. She didn't even mind the mistakes that much, when she'd have to unwind the yarn and start again.

Over and over again as she practiced her knitting, Iris's gaze returned to the closet door.

Finally she laid her work aside and went to the closet under the stairs. She opened the door. As it swung open, a draft blew in and shifted the coats on the rack.

Iris leaned in, peering into the shadows, then lowered herself to a sitting position. She shut the door behind her, leaving just a crack for light. Deep in the closet was a mirror that her dad still hadn't gotten around to hanging.

Iris had reported to Boris a while ago about her re-search into Mirror Gazing. "You have to wear loose cloth-ing," she'd told him, "and you're not supposed to wear any jewelry. Then you sit with something that reminds you of the person you've lost. And you look into the mir-ror, and after a while, if you concentrate and wait long enough, you're supposed to see the person."

Iris had shrugged, like she didn't really believe it would work, and then she'd dropped the subject. But here she was, and here was a mirror, and Sarah's tennis racket, and Iris's parents were both busy in other parts of the house. Iris took the cover off and laid the racket across her lap. She shifted the mirror against the wall so that she could stare right into her own eyes.

Iris waited, and waited, thrumming her fingers across the racket's strings. She didn't look at her hands, kept her gaze focused on her reflection. She longed to see Sarah's blue eyes gazing out at her, her reddish hair, her freckled nose. Her grin. But even in the midst of all that *wanting,* Iris remembered something else. A day not too long before Sarah died, when the two of them had stared together into the bathroom mirror at Iris's old house in Seal Beach.

"Your nose is longer than mine," Sarah said. "And your eyebrows are darker."

"But we have the same lips, almost," Iris said. "And our hair is the same length."

And they both wore bangs, and they liked the same strawberry-flavored lip balm. The similarities were greater than the differences, and Iris remembered that, on that day, she had felt that this was as close as she would ever get to having a sister.

Now, alone in the darkness, Iris's gaze focused on her own features. There was a scratch above her right eye, where Charles had stepped on her in the middle of the night. Her bangs were gone, grown out. And her eyes seemed darker, maybe wider, than they had once been. Maybe it was the half-light of the closet. Maybe it was time passing, or all the sadness she had felt in the past months. Maybe it was living with so much rain. Whatever it was, Iris saw that her face was not the same as the face she had compared with Sarah's, months and miles behind her. She was not the same.

She wanted so badly to see Sarah there in the mirror, beside her own reflection, or even within it. She wished so hard, again, that by a miracle, Sarah would be there.

Or even her ghost. Iris would be willing to settle for that.

She closed her eyes against everything—the racket in her hands, her image in the mirror, the shine of her tears. She would never stop wishing. She would never stop missing Sarah. She would never forget her birthdays, or the sound the ball made when it hit Sarah's racket just right. Iris knew she would never go back to the way she had been, before Sarah had died.

When she opened her eyes, Iris was not surprised to find that there had been no miracle reincarnation.

Sarah wasn't there. But her racket was. Iris ran her fingers again across its strings, and then held it against her chest. Finally she stood, and pushed open the door, and stepped back into the hallway. Gently, she closed the door behind her.

She blinked, waiting for her eyes to adjust to the light, and she tapped the edge of the racket's head against her palm, as Sarah had done, and spun it once, twice, three times, listening to the *whoosh* of air through its strings.

It was a beautiful racket. Still holding it, Iris went into the kitchen and called Boris. He answered on the third ring.

"Boris," Iris said, "do you know how to play tennis?"

"No way," he said. "That ball flying across the net at you as fast as the other person can hit it? Uh-uh."

Iris bounced the racket's strings against her knee. "Come on," she said. "Let me teach you how to play."

"I don't think so, Iris."

"Come on," she said again.

Boris was silent for a minute. Iris listened to him breathe. Finally he said, "You won't hit it hard?"

"I promise I'll be super careful," said Iris.

He sighed. "Okay," he said. "I'll try."

22

Out of the twelve eggs, eleven hatched. Iris's dad let her leave the last egg in the incubator for a whole week, but finally he told her it was time to return the incubator to the store in Portland.

"It would have hatched by now, Pigeon, if it was going to."

Iris knew he was right. She'd looked it up on the Internet. That last egg wasn't going to hatch.

"Can we bury it in the garden?" she asked.

"Absolutely. That way, when it decomposes, it'll feed the soil, and the soil will feed the plants, and the plants will feed us. So in a way, the egg will live even though it'll never hatch."

Iris liked that idea, the idea of the egg turning into something, of the egg not being nothing. She watched her dad unplug the incubator. The heating coils faded from bright yellow to orange-red. Some eggs won't hatch. That's just the way it is. Leaving them in the incubator for days and days couldn't make them hatch, no matter how badly she wanted it.

She watched as her father opened the incubator door, as he extracted the egg that would never be a chick, as the coils cooled to black.

Iris closed the incubator door.

As she walked into the kitchen, the constant, high-pitched, many-voiced "peep" grew louder. Corralled in a playpen in a corner of the kitchen, eleven chicks peeped all day, as long as there was light, only quieting when the sun went down.

She walked out the back door, took a shovel from the porch, followed her dad to the garden.

"Where do you want to bury the egg?" he asked.

Iris found a nice flat spot between the cabbage and the cauliflower, and she dug a little hole. The earth was soft from their earlier tilling, and the shovel cut easily through the dirt. Iris watched her dad set down the egg and tuck it into the ground. And then all she could think about was how that egg would never, ever hatch.

Everything made her cry, Iris thought, a little angry with herself. So many worse things could happen—so many worse things *had* happened, *did* happen, and here she was crying over one unhatched egg.

The thing was, they'd never know what might have been in that egg—maybe the friendliest little chicken ever laid should have cracked out, but didn't. And they'd never know *why* the egg hadn't hatched. Had it been jostled during transport? Was it somehow never fertilized in the first place? Was there something wrong with it, some genetic mutation that made life unfeasible?

Most of the eggs had hatched; this one would not. Boris had lived, but other babies with his same condition had not. Iris had survived; Sarah had not. Did God like some of the eggs better, or prefer Boris to the other unborn babies? Did the universe love Sarah less than Iris? Is that why Iris had been standing by the fence that day? Was that a miracle? Was Boris's survival, or the birth of a chick, a miracle?

Iris didn't know. She *couldn't* know, not really. Neither could Claude the psychic or the doctor who weighed the soul. Or Linus Pauling, who didn't think that miracles could happen, or Thomas Edison. All the people who listened to recorded static, searching for voices. Those nuns, the ones who were so sure that Boris had lived because of their prayers to the right dead pope—they didn't really know either. They *believed*. They *hoped*. But hoping, Iris decided, is not the same as *knowing*.

They would never have those answers. So Iris did what had to be done—she scooped a shovelful of dirt atop the egg. She patted the earth down hard and flat. She turned away.

But before she left the garden, she saw something nearby, something so small she nearly missed it, something she might have expected to see, but hadn't— sprouts, tiny and green, like blades of grass, but aligned in a neat row just where she and her parents had planted seeds.

"Dad," she said. "Look!"

He did, and then he looked back at Iris. A wide bright grin split his beard. "Will you look at that, Pigeon!"

Iris knelt down and ran her finger across the fine green tips. They bent gently beneath her touch, then sprang back up.

"What'd we plant here, do you remember?"

"Broccoli, I think."

"Well, it looks like we're going to need a lot of cheese sauce," said her dad.

They walked together carefully through the garden, eyes on the ground. And they saw more sprouts—radish greens, the twining start of pea shoots. With each discovery they pointed and laughed, calling to each other. Pushing up all around them—beautiful green beginnings.

It wasn't until they started to head back toward the house that Iris realized she had forgotten to put on her raincoat. Her sweatshirt was damp, and she was sort of cold, but she wasn't frozen through and miserable.

"Hey, Dad," she said. "It's raining."

"What's new?" He laughed.

"It's raining, and I didn't even notice," Iris said. "*That's* new." She stopped and spread out her arms, turned her face up to the sky. Down came the rain, drop after drop, splattering her cheeks and running down her neck, under the collar of her sweatshirt.

She began to turn, slowly at first, and then faster and faster until she was spinning, until she was dizzy, until up and down lost meaning, until all she could think about was the motion that carried her into her turn, and the way her feet slip-slid in the mud.

She caught sight of her dad. He'd dropped the shovel and was spinning too, his face turned up to catch the rain.

Bad things happen, Iris thought. *People die. Eggs sometimes do not hatch. But miracles . . . they happen too.*

There were miracles all around her, right in this very moment. There was a miracle in spinning with her dad, under the heavy sky. In the sun that peeked through the gilt-edged clouds. There was a miracle in their crops that bravely emerged from the soil into the big wide world. In the chicks, peeping in the kitchen.

And, Iris thought, if she could actually teach Boris to play a decent game of tennis, that would be miraculous.

She stumbled to a stop and fell into her dad. He picked her up and hugged her close. Then he spun once more, this time with her in his arms. She felt the now-familiar scratch of his beard against her cheek; she smelled the memory of the fire he built each day in the flannel of his shirt.

Clean, fresh rain showered down on them.

There was a miracle, too, in that.

Acknowledgments

The Question of Miracles would not exist if not for Rubin Pfeffer, who challenged me to write a middle grade novel. It is such a pleasure, Rubin Pfeffer, to be your client and your friend.

Adah Nuchi, I feel like a racehorse who has been ridden by the finest jockey. You knew where to push further and when to pull back, and you softened my instinct to race full speed and full force to help me create something much finer. You really, truly are a wonderful editor. I'm so glad to have found a home with Houghton Mifflin Harcourt.

My wonderful family of readers—Nana, Dad, Sasha, Mischa, and Zak—as before, your support is incalculable. Keith, I am grateful as always that you value my writing time above silly things like laundry and a clean house. And Max, Davis, and Kaycee, my middle grade editors . . . your willing ears and wonderful advice helped shape Iris's story. Thank you.

David King, source of all things Magic, I so appreciate your expert insight. I can't wait to see my name in the list of acknowledgments in *your* novel!

Huge thanks to Kate, for all of your help with the medical and religious backstory. And, of course, a special acknowledgment to Declan, the Boy Who Lived.

Don't miss

Odette has a list: Things That Aren't Fair. At the top of the list is her parents' decision to take the family on the road in an ugly RV they've nicknamed the Coach. There's nothing fair about leaving California and living in the Coach with her parents and exasperating brother. And there's definitely nothing fair about Grandma Sissy's failing zhealth, and the painful realities and difficult decisions that come with it. Most days it seems as if everything in Odette's life is far from fair—but does it have to be?

Turn the page for a sneak peek of *Far from Fair*.

The Ugliest Thing

I T WAS THE ugliest thing she had ever seen. Obnoxiously ugly. Embarrassingly ugly. Epically ugly. And it was sitting in her family's driveway.

Actually, no. It was sitting in the Waldmans' driveway—or, at least, what would shortly become the Waldmans' driveway when escrow closed in a few days and the house Odette Zyskowski grew up in wouldn't be her home anymore. That *thing* would be her home. That run-down, beat-up brown and brown RV that Mom and Dad had just pulled up in, honking what was intended to be a cheerful beep, but instead sounded like the mournful death cry of a desperate whale.

Odette looked behind herself at the house, trying to ignore the SOLD banner splashed across the FOR SALE sign stuck in the front lawn. She had never given the house much thought. It was just a house. But now she saw the brick path winding through the grass from the sidewalk, uneven and tipsy, and it occurred to Odette that she knew every brick on that path—which ones were chipped, which listed slightly to the side, which were stamped with the bricklayer's name, Steinberg & Sons.

She saw the bright red front door, the door she slammed through every afternoon at 3:14 p.m. Behind that door, Odette knew, was the mud bench where she ditched her backpack and shoes. She saw the wide, bright windows, the shutters that framed them. She took in the dark shingle roof that her parents had been talking about replacing for years but would soon become the Waldmans' problem.

It was a beautiful home.

Mom cut the engine of the RV, and Dad threw open the metal door on the side and a set of two steps popped out.

Rex stood next to Odette, rocking up onto the balls of his feet, the way he did when he got excited. "Awesome, awesome, awesome," he chanted to himself, and when Dad called, "So, what do you guys think?" Rex shouted "Awesome!" and ran full speed into Dad, butting his head into Dad's stomach and grinding it against him.

Dad said "Oof!" and laughed, and Mom, coming out of the RV, said, "Careful, buddy," and then she asked Odette, "So, honey, what do you think?" but Odette was already heading back into the Waldmans' house, slamming the red door shut behind her.

Hands

ODETTE'S ROOM WAS at the end of the hall, just before the turn to her parents' bedroom. The hall was stacked with boxes, piled three high and labeled in thick black Sharpie ink: REX'S ROOM (STORAGE); LINENS AND BEDDING (STORAGE); BATHROOM MISC (YARD SALE); BOOKS (LIBRARY GIVEAWAY); BATHROOM ESSENTIALS (COACH).

That was what Mom was calling the RV: the "Coach." The word brought a few things to Odette's mind—baseball, for one, a sport she found endlessly boring but still somehow comforting; Mr. Santiago, the track-and-field coach at Odette's middle school, who after he'd seen her run the mile in PE had spent most of Odette's sixth grade year trying to recruit her to the team; and Cinderella's pumpkin-turned-coach that she took to the ball.

None of these images had anything to do with Mom's

use of the word in sentences like "When we pick up the Coach, the first thing we'll do is fix up your private space, Detters" (which was what she liked to call Odette), and "It might not look like much in the pictures, kids, but the Coach has under twenty thousand miles on it and is as snug as a bug inside."

The Coach. Sitting in the driveway. Odette couldn't get far enough away, no matter how good a runner she was. So she had to content herself with slamming her bedroom door—hard enough to make the windows rattle—and throwing herself face-down onto the bed.

Her sheets smelled like home. The same detergent her mom had been using as long as Odette had been aware of detergent smell. Probably before that. And even with her eyes closed and her face pressed into her bedspread, Odette could perfectly picture her room. The pale blue walls. The light pink ceiling, a gently whirling fan just above her bed. The windows, looking out over the back-yard, with their gossamer-thin ballooning white curtains.

And more: the seven pillows she arranged each morn-ing after making her bed, and then restacked each night on the carpet before climbing between her sheets. Two yellow, one pink, one green, two blue, one red.

There wouldn't be room for her seven throw pillows in the Coach. "You can bring one," Mom had told her.

One. Absolutely ridiculous.

When the knock came at her door, Odette ignored it. She knew it was Dad from the way he knocked—always a little pattern, a little song, not just straight across with all his knuckles.

She heard him open the door anyway, even though she hadn't said "Come in," and that bothered her too, that lack of respect, that lack of privacy, and the mean little voice in her head taunted, *You'd better get used to it, Odette. There won't be much privacy in the Coach.*

Her dad cleared his throat. Odette could tell that he was still lurking just inside the doorway. That was her dad—a lurker. He was always ho-ing and hum-ing about decisions, weighing the costs and benefits. Mom sometimes said, "You're going to drive me crazy, Simon! Just *do* something!"

But he didn't usually do *anything*—at least, not anything important. He'd ho and hum until Odette's mom got tired of waiting and just did it herself—whatever it was that needed doing. Choosing which car to buy. Picking the toppings for the pizza.

And then, three months ago, Odette's dad had *done something*. Something big. Something crazy.

"They were going to lay off three guys," she heard Dad telling Mom. "Three guys who actually *like* their jobs. And with Sissy being so sick, not to mention the trouble we've been having with us ... with each other ... I thought, well, I guess I thought it couldn't make things any worse."

It was late at night, and Dad hadn't gotten home from the office in time for dinner, which wasn't that unusual. Odette was supposed to be asleep, like Rex was in his room (dark blue with deep-sea ocean fish painted on the walls and a jellyfish diorama on his bookcase), but she wasn't. She was sneaking out to the kitchen for a cookie. And there were her parents, sitting at the table, with only the small sink light turned on. They were holding hands.

It looked so strange, their hands. Fingers interwoven, like the kids at school, like they were announcing to the world that they were a couple. It wasn't something Odette was used to seeing between her parents. Usually, if anyone was holding anyone's hand, it was Mom and Rex. Sometimes Dad and Rex. But never Mom and Dad.

Odette had backed slowly down the hall toward her room. What did that mean, to lay someone off? And what did Dad mean, that whatever he had done couldn't make things any worse?

Odette knew Grandma Sissy wasn't healthy. Not that Mom and Dad had told her all the details, but Odette knew. She'd heard Mom on the phone with Grandma Sissy, asking about doctor appointments and pain medication and nausea. But that other thing that Dad had said, about trouble between him and Mom . . . Odette didn't know what to think about that.

When she woke up the next morning, she had forgotten all about the night before, the table, the handholding. And she walked into the kitchen ready to find what she always found: Rex expounding about something that fascinated him—queer ocean life, or rare types of pygmy animals that were legal to own as pets, or the best way to make applesauce—and her mother nodding and pretending to listen while making their breakfast and packing their lunches.

Instead she found them—her parents—sitting again at the table, holding hands. Holding hands, again. For a minute she thought they hadn't moved, but then she saw that Mom was dressed, not in her robe, and that Dad was wearing his weekend clothes instead of the rumpled suit he'd been in last night, even though this was a Thursday. And Rex was with them, eating oatmeal and whacking his feet against the bottom of the table in a rhythmic thumping beat that sounded to Odette the way a zombie might sound dragging a non-working leg behind himself.

And then Dad had smiled—something else she hadn't seen much of lately, come to think of it, and Mom said, "Good morning, Detters," and then they proceeded to ruin her life.

Not Okay

"YOU WANT TO talk, Odette?" asked Dad.

She shook her head into the bedspread, still refusing to look up.

He sighed. Odette imagined him shifting his weight, leaning against her door frame.

"No," she said into the mattress.

There was a pause. Then he said, "It's going to be okay, honey. I promise." More lurking, and then Odette heard him walk away. He left the door open.

Odette sighed and flipped onto her back. She was beginning to feel smothered, face-down on her bed. The house was hot.

The Coach has air conditioning! Odette could imagine Mom's peppy response.

Dad promised it would be okay. He *promised.* As if

he had that kind of authority. That kind of pull with the universe. Odette knew a lie when she heard one. How on earth could he know everything would be okay? To Odette, it was clear as a glass of water that things were *not* okay. Not by a mile.

ELANA K. ARNOLD completed her MA in creative writing at the University of California, Davis. She grew up in Southern California, where she was lucky enough to have a family who let her read as many books as she wanted. She is the author of several young adult novels as well as the middle grade novels *The Question of Miracles* and *Far from Fair*. She lives in Huntington Beach, California, with her husband, two children, and a menagerie of animals. Visit her website at **www.elanakarnold.com**.